Bolan leapt to the driver's side of the truck bed

He reached around to the open window of the cab for a handhold, then swung himself along the driver's-side door, standing on the running board. The hardman gaped in surprise, instant reflexes snapping his elbow at the gripping hand. But without enough leverage, the blow was ineffective and the Executioner's grip held. He fired the Desert Eagle into the driver's neck.

The truck swerved off the road toward a ravine. Bolan transferred his grip from the window to the steering wheel and yanked the vehicle back onto the asphalt.

Wedging a grenade under one of the canvas's rope restraints, he pulled the pin and jumped into the void. As he hit the ground an explosion rumbled all around him, and his vision was filled with a bright burning light. Where the truck had been was a patch of smoking, charred earth.

With a squeal of brakes the Suburban came to a rocking halt fifty feet away. Jiahua stepped out of the vehicle. "You okay, Belasko?"

"Yeah. I'll live. This'll get their attention."

MACK BOLAN ®

The Executioner

#152 Combat Stretch
#153 Firebase Florida
#154 Night Hit
#155 Hawaiian Heat
#156 Phantom Force
#157 Cayman Strike
#158 Firing Line
#159 Steel and Flame
#160 Storm Warning
#161 Eye of the Storm
#162 Colors of Hell
#163 Warrior's Edge
#164 Death Trail
#165 Fire Sweep
#166 Assassin's Creed
#167 Double Action
#168 Blood Price
#169 White Heat
#170 Baja Blitz
#171 Deadly Force
#172 Fast Strike
#173 Capitol Hit
#174 Battle Plan
#175 Battle Ground
#176 Ransom Run
#177 Evil Code
#178 Black Hand
#179 War Hammer
#180 Force Down
#181 Shifting Target
#182 Lethal Agent
#183 Clean Sweep
#184 Death Warrant
#185 Sudden Fury
#186 Fire Burst
#187 Cleansing Flame

#188 War Paint
#189 Wellfire
#190 Killing Range
#191 Extreme Force
#192 Maximum Impact
#193 Hostile Action
#194 Deadly Contest
#195 Select Fire
#196 Triburst
#197 Armed Force
#198 Shoot Down
#199 Rogue Agent
#200 Crisis Point
#201 Prime Target
#202 Combat Zone
#203 Hard Contact
#204 Rescue Run
#205 Hell Road
#206 Hunting Cry
#207 Freedom Strike
#208 Death Whisper
#209 Asian Crucible
#210 Fire Lash
#211 Steel Claws
#212 Ride the Beast
#213 Blood Harvest
#214 Fission Fury
#215 Fire Hammer

DON PENDLETON'S
THE EXECUTIONER®
FIRE HAMMER

A GOLD EAGLE BOOK FROM
WORLDWIDE®

TORONTO • NEW YORK • LONDON
AMSTERDAM • PARIS • SYDNEY • HAMBURG
STOCKHOLM • ATHENS • TOKYO • MILAN
MADRID • WARSAW • BUDAPEST • AUCKLAND

First edition November 1996
ISBN 0-373-64215-6

Special thanks and acknowledgment to
Tim Somheil for his contribution to this work.

FIRE HAMMER

Printed in U.S.A.

If peace and survival are to be achieved, the search must almost certainly go beyond the effort to find a balance in thermonuclear terror.

—John Kenneth Galbraith
The Affluent Society (1958)

Every two-bit nation with money to spend is developing nuclear weapons. This is dangerous. But help is on the way. I'll make certain of it.

—Mack Bolan

THE
MACK BOLAN®
LEGEND

Nothing less than a war could have fashioned the destiny of the man called Mack Bolan. Bolan earned the Executioner title in the jungle hell of Vietnam.

But this soldier also wore another name—Sergeant Mercy. He was so tagged because of the compassion he showed to wounded comrades-in-arms and Vietnamese civilians.

Mack Bolan's second tour of duty ended prematurely when he was given emergency leave to return home and bury his family, victims of the Mob. Then he declared a one-man war against the Mafia.

He confronted the Families head-on from coast to coast, and soon a hope of victory began to appear. But Bolan had broken society's every rule. That same society started gunning for this elusive warrior—to no avail.

So Bolan was offered amnesty to work within the system against terrorism. This time, as an employee of Uncle Sam, Bolan became Colonel John Phoenix. With a command center at Stony Man Farm in Virginia, he and his new allies—Able Team and Phoenix Force—waged relentless war on a new adversary: the KGB.

But when his one true love, April Rose, died at the hands of the Soviet terror machine, Bolan severed all ties with Establishment authority.

Now, after a lengthy lone-wolf struggle and much soul-searching, the Executioner has agreed to enter an "arm's-length" alliance with his government once more, reserving the right to pursue personal missions in his Everlasting War.

1

A constant rush of noise came from the traffic on the interstate highway beyond the office building. Otherwise the parking lot and corporate park were silent. It was nearly 9:00 p.m., and the building itself was dark except for two offices, one of which belonged to Hank Chiang.

A figure in black stood in the shadows, watching the building. A casual observer wouldn't have known he was there. After a long minute the dark figure moved across the lot, reappearing at the darkened rear utility door. Reaching into a duffel slung on his back, he withdrew a set of slim steel tools. A moment later the door was unlocked and opened.

Mack Bolan felt exposed once he was inside. The problem was he didn't know for sure if the attackers were within the building yet.

Hal Brognola had reached him just an hour earlier, an edge to his voice that almost made him sound frantic: go to Lisle, Illinois, to the headquarters of EastStar Corporation, locate the chief executive officer, Hang "Hank" Chiang and protect and detain him. The Chinese, Brognola warned, were on their way.

"Chiang's got Intel that'll save lots of lives," the big Fed had said. "Most importantly he knows where a Chinese terrorist group called CLAAC is based. We think CLAAC has got an agenda that includes genocide and nuclear blackmail.

"We've got to keep Chiang alive at all costs," were his last words. "All other considerations are secondary."

Bolan wished he'd had time to get more facts, but Brognola had clearly communicated the need for speed. He'd accepted the assignment and left immediately.

He found the first floor deserted and headed up the stairs, hand on the butt of his Beretta 93-R as it nestled in its shoulder rig under his jacket. The second and third floors were also empty: expansive, carpeted offices silent and lit only by emergency-exit signs and the occasional security light.

Two offices on the fourth floor were illuminated and Bolan watched from the window of the stairwell door for a long minute before proceeding. When he stepped into the hallway, he heard conversation. The first office was empty. Bolan assumed its occupant was one of the conversants down the hall, where he should find Hank Chiang. A glance out the window showed him a Lincoln Towncar limousine, a black Econoliner van and a large panel truck pulling into the lot.

Bolan knew in his gut it was the Chinese. They cruised to the main door of the building, and men with distinctively Asian features began to get out of all three vehicles. At least ten men streamed from the panel truck before it pulled around the corner, presumably to guard the rear of the building.

The Chinese had arrived, but they hadn't sent the hit man Brognola had anticipated. They'd sent an army. If he hadn't realized this was a big deal before, Bolan would have been convinced of it now. Somebody was willing to invest a large amount of intelligence resources to make sure Chiang became very dead.

And it was Bolan's job to ensure it didn't happen, however outgunned he was.

The two men down the hall were still conversing, unaware of the imminent assault. Bolan couldn't risk getting trapped in that office with them. He'd have to attack from the rear. He stepped across the hall, into a dark office, once again slipping into shadow.

THE ARMY DEPLOYED wordlessly, the first group of assassins heading for an elevator. Without a word they ascended, metal clicks the only sounds as semiautomatic-weapon safeties disengaged, followed by an electronic tone announcing the car's arrival on the fourth floor and the squeak of the doors pulling open.

The four disembarked and stood in the hall as the doors of the second elevator opened. Three more men exited, while several others began emerging from the stairwell. Together they advanced down the hallway, investigating empty offices as they went.

The Executioner listened to them coming, stepping behind the office door as it opened. The scarred face of a Chinese agent examined the office, then glanced around the door. Bolan shot him in the forehead with the silenced Beretta.

He grabbed the corpse by the collar even as it was slumping and dragged it around the door, then he stepped into the open. The Beretta spit three more times into three Chinese agents, and they collapsed to the floor in a heap.

Bolan dived over the bodies, landing on the floor inside another dark room, even as the Chinese discovered they were under attack. Instantly semiautomatic rifle fire ripped up the walls and the doorway of the office Bolan had emerged from. He'd been lucky enough to strike at the tail end of the Chinese force, and the survivors hadn't seen him maneuver into the other office. He bounded to his feet and drew the Desert Eagle as he faced the hall again. The doorway he'd just left was disintegrating under heavy fire. He edged into sight of the Chinese and fired the Desert Eagle, the explosive impact of the .44 Magnum bullets flinging two of the hit men into the others.

The soldier pulled back in time to avoid return fire. He grabbed a gas mask from his duffel and dragged it onto his head, then withdrew a high-explosive smoke grenade. He fired out the door, the Desert Eagle's .44 rounds creating lunarlike craters in the hallway walls, then stepped to the door, pulled the pin on the HE and lobbed the bomb.

The eruption was substantial in the confines of the offices, and the oily black smoke seemed to fill the atmosphere. Bolan pulled the mask over his face and stepped into the hall after a quick five-count. The Chinese were choking and blinded, and one staggered in his direction through the cloud, trying to aim his weapon. The Executioner drilled him through the chest, and he collapsed.

The door to Chiang's office, located at a ninety-degree turn in the hall, was closed. The rest of the Chinese hardmen had escaped in the other direction—Bolan could hear them gasping for breath—unless some had made it into Chiang's office prior to the explosion. He tried the door, found it locked and shot it out. A round from the Desert Eagle destroyed the doorknob and sprang the door, which Bolan kicked savagely and stepped through, sweeping the room. He saw no Chinese hitters, just two businessmen. One was slumped in a chair with the back of his skull blown off. The other stood behind the desk, sighting a Smith & Wesson Model 57.

The soldier could have easily killed the man before he had time to shoot the handgun. Instead, he retreated into the hall, drawing the Beretta as the bullet blasted through the doorway where he had been standing. He stepped into the office again and loosed one round, the Smith & Wesson jumping out of the businessman's hand.

The man swore and sucked his finger.

"You Hank Chiang?" Bolan asked.

"Yeah. Who the hell are you?"

"I'm here to help you elude your friends in the hall. Is there another way out of here?"

"No!"

"Why did you shoot that man?"

Chiang grimaced. "He had information I couldn't afford to let fall into the wrong hands."

"They aren't here to kidnap anyone." Bolan was frustrated again at how much he didn't know about the situation he was in. Furthermore, it was obvious the man he had been sent to protect seemed by no means an innocent himself. He'd just murdered his co-worker in cold blood.

The only way out was the way he'd come in. The Chinese had withdrawn from the gas cloud, and maybe some of them had managed to avoid getting a strong dose. There was every chance the attackers would be able to trap Bolan and Chiang in the office until reinforcements arrived to take them out.

Gunshots rang out, and the door hinge shattered. The reinforcements had already arrived. Three more Chinese appeared from the direction of the elevator, through the dissipating smoke. Two sported automatic weapons, the last a fully automatic M-16. Chiang fell behind his desk, and Bolan sank to one knee, firing three rounds into the approaching death squad. They dropped one after another, but not before the soldier felt the burning breath of a .22 round whizzing over his head. The last gunner to fall lay jerking on the floor, spasmodically firing off continuous rounds from the M-16, mutilating the corpse next to him.

Bolan fired again, taking off the top of the man's head, then edged to the door, looking in the other direction of the L-shaped hallway. Figures were mustering in the thinning smoke. The soldier cursed the overly effective air-exchange system in the office building. He took a moment to drop the Eagle's clip and ram home a fresh one, then rattled off six rounds at the approaching figures. He'd hit at least a couple of them but could only guess how many were still able-bodied.

"Chiang!"

The businessman had found his Smith & Wesson on the carpet and was inspecting it for damage.

"Come on!"

Chiang approached the door reluctantly. Bolan raised the Beretta and cut loose, sweeping the smoky hallway in a deadly figure eight. He grabbed Chiang by the suit collar and dragged him into the hall, flinging the man in the direction of the stairs.

"Go."

Chiang laughed nervously. "You're crazy!"

Bolan didn't like dealing with civilians. He fired another burst down the hall and prodded Chiang with his foot. The man stumbled in the direction of the stairs, and the soldier stepped after him, trying to keep an eye in both directions at once while maintaining a steady suppressing fire. He knew he was just a step ahead of the Chinese at this point—a lead he had to maintain if there was any hope of getting out alive with his less-than-cooperative partner. He holstered the Desert Eagle and grabbed the M-16 out of the dead man's grip. It might prove useful.

He jumped into the stairwell ahead of Chiang, firing a burst at the dark-haired gunner racing up the stairs. The force of the rounds threw the target backward onto the lower landing, where he sprawled in an untidy heap.

Bolan checked the hall again and found a Chinese hitter on his hands and knees crawling toward the stairwell with a small chromed automatic pistol in one hand and a walkie-talkie in the other, shouting into it. The soldier fired off a round, drilling the bullet through both the walkie-talkie and the assassin just as the man was ready to return fire. No one else was visible.

The Executioner headed down the stairs, dragging Chiang behind him. They jumped over the body at the third floor, Bolan holstering the Beretta. When they reached the second-floor landing, he slammed through the door, sweeping the room with the M-16. Empty. He yanked the red fire-alarm device on the wall, and the building filled with raucous buzzing.

"What did you do that for?"

"When the fire department gets here, it won't take them long to call the police. The Chinese will definitely want to have cleared the scene by then. They now have a limited amount of time to hunt us down."

"You've narrowed their odds."

"Yeah."

"Do you think they'll still have time to find us?"

"Sure. But at the moment they've lost us. Maybe we can keep a step ahead of them. Meanwhile, I want some facts, Chiang. Most importantly I want to know where CLAAC is based."

The Chinese businessman was startled when Bolan used the acronym, and he laughed nervously. "I bet you would! Who are you, anyway?"

"That's not important right now. What *is* important is that I'm saving your life."

Behind them the elevator binged. "You haven't yet, mister!" Chiang cried.

Bolan moved quickly among the office partitions, dragging his companion to an east-side window. A single guard stood at the back doorway Bolan had used to enter the building. Directly below their window was the tall, boxy panel truck, which could possibly hold more Chinese hardmen.

There was no way to do it quietly, so Bolan acted as quickly as possible. He blasted through the tempered glass with a half-dozen rounds from the M-16, attracting the attention of the guard below. The soldier fired a 3-round burst into the sentry's shoulder, sending him flopping to the ground, his AR-15 clattering beside him. There was no doubt the rifle fire would have alerted the Chinese at the front of the building. Bolan had just seconds.

It was an eight-foot drop to the top of the panel truck. He ordered Chiang through the window, but the man protested. Bolan had no time to argue. He moved the M-16 to his other hand and drew the Beretta.

"Jump or I shoot you dead where you stand."

"You can't kill me," Chiang said, a look of panic on his face. "You're here to save me!"

"Out the window!" Chiang scurried to obey. He crawled onto the ledge and peered down at the top of the panel truck, whimpering. Bolan rammed a shoulder against Chiang's back, and the man dropped onto the roof of the panel truck.

The sound of Chiang landing on the roof was what the occupants of the truck had been waiting for. The doors on either side of the cab opened, and the driver almost stepped on Chiang as the man flopped from the truck roof to the pavement. The driver aimed a .22 handgun at the stunned man gasping for breath at his feet. The gunner who had exited on the passenger side leveled a rifle at Bolan's face, which was framed in the gaping hole that had been the second-floor window.

Bolan considered his next move. He had two choices: kill the driver before the driver shot Chiang, or shoot the passenger before the passenger shot at him.

He didn't know who Chiang was or why he was important, but he knew he had taken an instant dislike to the abrasive, murderous company head. On the other hand, Brognola believed there were vital reasons to keep Chiang alive, which involved saving a number of innocent lives.

The Executioner aimed carefully at the driver and blew away a section of his skull with a 9 mm parabellum round a fraction of a second before the man would have shot Chiang. The other gunner's auto rifle fired in the same instant and Bolan felt the bullet tear through his clothing and burn the flesh of his neck, just above the collarbone. A burst from the M-16 drilled through the rifleman's chest, pitching him onto his back.

Bolan dived out the window, aware that an unknown number of Chinese were approaching from the rear, and heard the shattering of glass as rifle fire exploded the last shards in the window. He somersaulted onto the roof of the truck, then righted himself.

"Get up," he ordered Chiang. Leveling the M-16 at the window he'd just exited, he fired off a quick burst. Pursuit would be slowed for a moment.

Chiang shoved off the corpse with obvious effort, and got to his feet.

"You drive," Bolan said.

The businessman hastened to comply, easing himself into the driver's seat. Bolan knelt in position on the truck roof, scanning all directions, and was ready when the first pair of Chinese gunmen ran around the corner. The M-16 cut through them at stomach height, shaking them like rag dolls, then dropping them to the ground like so much scrap meat.

The muzzle of a weapon appeared around the corner and sighted on the truck as Chiang hit the gas. Bolan crouched low on the roof for balance and fired at the corner. With a flash of scarlet the gun dropped to the ground along with the crumbling brick that had been part of the building.

"Get us out of here!" Bolan shouted. The truck lurched forward with a surprising burst of speed, heading toward the south side of the building. A hardman without a hand screamed and writhed in the parking lot. Two other Chinese gunners spotted the van and brought their pistols into target acquisition.

As Bolan started to cut loose with the M-16, the panel truck braked hard, flipping him onto the hood and slamming him to the blacktop. The impact was so powerful that he lay stunned for a moment, but then the truck surged directly at him. He jumped to the side on his hands and knees and sprang to his feet, feeling the wind of the vehicle passing inches from his body. The truck slammed over the curb, bullets peppering the metal, then bounced onto the street, escaping.

The Executioner had no time to contemplate the betrayal as the enemy gunners began to close in. He triggered the M-16, which ceased to function abruptly. The two nearest gunners toppled before he turned to flee, diving behind a steel garbage container at the edge of the lot. The night was filled with the metallic thunder of bullets punching into his cover. Another sound shattered the night air—sirens. It had been just minutes since Bolan pulled the alarm, and the local fire department was reacting quickly.

The fire truck roared into sight down the street—a massive hook-and-ladder vehicle, flashing lights stabbing into the darkness. Bolan was sure the Chinese hardmen weren't going to have any qualms about killing firemen in their attempts to make a clean getaway. He was determined to save as many of their innocent lives as possible. But once the truck got in range...

He leveled the Desert Eagle at the approaching fire truck and fired carefully. The driver's-side mirror turned into a mass of dangling metal, and the truck slammed to a halt, still a block away. It began maneuvering in the narrow street for a way to escape.

Bolan's situation hadn't improved. He was still stuck in the open without an escape route in sight.

He heard a scream from the truck, and a fire fighter tumbled to the street and was still. Bolan scanned for the sniper—there was a gunman on the fourth floor. The soldier stood over the top of the garbage container for an unobstructed view of the fourth floor. But he was dangerously exposed for the moment it took to aim and fire. There was no gap between the noise of the shot from the Desert Eagle and the sound of a fresh barrage hitting his shield. He huddled down again, momentarily satisfied at having seen the fourth-floor gunman kneel and crumple.

More sirens announced the arrival of the police, called by the fire department. Bolan didn't need the police any more than he needed the Chinese. The cops probably wouldn't try to kill him, but they'd arrest him and lock him up until Brognola pulled the requisite strings.

The barrage of bullets against the garbage container halted, and Bolan crept around its far side. The fourth-floor window had remained empty, and it appeared as if the Chinese were moving out. He had a clear shot at the last two, one of them the man with the shot-off hand, just before they ran around the corner to the building front. He didn't take it. Instead, he bolted across the empty lot and slammed his back into the wall, the Desert Eagle ready to take on anybody who had spotted him. But at the moment he was alone. He could make his way to the abandoned rear of the building, up the incline and across the interstate, and be home free.

As the hook-and-ladder truck maneuvered its massive bulk in an attempt to retreat, the windshield pebbled and the driver slumped onto the steering wheel. The Chinese were picking off firemen from the front of the building.

Without conscious decision the Executioner abandoned his plan of escape, dropping to his hands and knees into the shrubbery that lined the building. He crawled to the front and through the foliage saw the Towncar and Econoliner waiting, engines running, with three Chinese gunmen standing guard. The soldier's first move was to ensure his cover—he carefully squeezed shots into the two closest parking-lot lights. The lamps exploded too quickly to provide clues to the guards as to the origin of the shots, and they didn't even consider the low mass of shrubbery against the building. Bolan aimed carefully through the dense leaves and picked them off slowly. The man in the middle spun helplessly as his two comrades clutched their bodies and fell, and he dropped to the ground for cover from an assailant he couldn't locate. A third round from the Beretta got him in the head even as he was descending, and all three guards were stilled.

Creeping to the front entrance, Bolan heard the sound of a quick approach from inside. The doors slammed open, and he fired from his crouch into the ankle of the first man out. The wounded man's momentum carried him onto his face against the concrete walk with a cry, two of his companions emerging before they realized what had happened.

One man dropped to the ground with a parabellum round in his forehead. From his crouched position Bolan saw the last gunner home in on him in the shrubbery. He had already switched the Beretta over to 3-round-burst mode, and he blasted through the thick veil of leaves, watching three well-grouped stains appear over the gunman's sternum. The corpse's skull cracked against the concrete when it fell, louder than the gunshots that had killed it.

Terrified, the man with the wounded ankle began to crawl away from the scene of death. He'd forgotten his gun, so Bolan let him flee. A last gunner ran from the building and stood among the ruin of his former comrades for only a second before diving for cover behind the limo.

Bolan rose from the foliage and put two holes into the vehicle, one on either side of the last man. The gunner turned and made the mistake of bringing his .38-caliber pistol into play, receiving as punishment a 9 mm bullet in his throat. Sitting down heavily, he gasped for breath three times before he died.

The Executioner crawled back into the shrubbery and along the front of the building until he reached the north end, where there were no lights and no parking lot, only the overgrown incline that ascended to Interstate 88. He crept along, putting the building between himself and the emergency vehicles. Even if anybody saw him make his escape, the police wouldn't be keen about rushing after him—not with the extent of the carnage he'd left behind.

He glanced back in time to see the last Chinese agent staggering onto his feet and raising his hands in the air as four squad cars made a semicircle around him and several officers trained their handguns on him. That man would have a lot of explaining to do, and not just to the local police, but to some high-level officials in the People's Republic.

He wasn't the only one with some explaining to do, Bolan thought, wincing as the pain in the wound above his collarbone finally sprang to life. The soldier wanted to know a lot more about this Hank Chiang and what exactly he was involved in. He intended to get a lot more from Hal Brognola as soon as he got a secure line to Stony Man Farm.

2

Hal Brognola groaned at Bolan's report and muttered something about "a disaster," then added, "we need a face-to-face immediately."

"Fine," Bolan replied. "Name the place."

"I'll come to you. Get a room at the Hyatt Regency O'Hare—you'll be within ten minutes of the airport. I'll meet you in the lobby at 4:00 a.m."

The big Fed rang off before Bolan had time to do more than grunt affirmatively. Brognola was rarely gruff, which meant something big was going down.

He took a taxi to his rented car, then drove to the convention hotel near the world's busiest airport. A reservation waited for him under the name Mike Belasko, an alias he often used and hadn't yet been forced to abandon.

There was no middle-of-the-night commercial flight from Washington D.C., to Chicago, which meant Brognola had arranged for a private jet. He wasn't the type to allocate such special services except in extreme instances. Bolan couldn't get away from the feeling that something big was coming down, something Brognola didn't trust even over secure phone lines.

There was nothing Bolan could do but be patient and get himself prepared for a quick start on whatever the task was when it was set before him. He showered and cleaned the wound above his collarbone. It was shallow and would heal quickly, but would probably add a scar to his collection. He ate a room-service meal, then organized his duffel and fieldstripped the Beretta and Desert Eagle.

SNAPPING AWAKE, Bolan was sitting up in bed before the phone completed its first ring. As he lifted the receiver, he saw it was 3:05 a.m., meaning he'd slept three hours. Brognola had made even better time than expected.

"I'm at the last lounge table in the lobby. Bring your gear."

He took the glass elevator down and spotted the familiar figure sitting at a table in the nearly empty lobby. The big Fed hardly glanced up when Bolan sank into the low, overstuffed chair, but slid a single black-and-white glossy photograph across to him.

An unfamiliar Oriental man about Bolan's age, gaunt and grim, peered from the photo with devious eyes.

"His name's Kao Lung. He lived in China until recently and heads a radical Chinese anti-Communist group called CLAAC. He hasn't exactly mixed in your circles." Brognola gazed at him from under his eyebrows and gave him two more black-and-white shots. "I think you'll soon be mixing in his. This is Steven Sellers. The other guy you've met."

The photo of Sellers showed the face of a haggard man in his fifties with drooping flesh and wisps of gray, unkempt hair—a man grown old before his time. The other photo was of Hank Chiang.

"Steven Sellers is a nuclear scientist. He began working for EastStar Corporation ten years ago after getting kicked out of two other jobs. He's a genius, but careless. He worked with radioactive material without regard for the usual protective measures, and as a result exposed a number of assistants to dangerous levels of radioactivity. Several got cancer. A couple died."

"Nice guy. How did he survive?" Bolan asked.

"Maybe he was careful when it came to protecting himself. Who knows? But Chiang got hold of him. At EastStar he oversaw purification of radioactive substances at the labs in Downers Grove, just a few miles from the headquarters you visited this evening, reporting directly to Chiang."

"Purification of radioactive substances for what purposes?"

"It's used in low-grade radioactive dyes with medicinal uses," Brognola replied. "That kind of stuff. Nothing sinister about it, but he was falling into his old habits of shoddy safety measures, which Chiang encouraged—it cut costs to the bone. They worked out a scam. Sellers reported the costs of these nonexistent safety measures to the corporation, which paid for them. Chiang arranged for the accounting and skimmed the cash."

"Very nice. But you haven't come here to tell me about an embezzlement scheme."

"No, I haven't. Chiang controlled the upper-level hierarchy at EastStar, but some of the lower-level types threatened to call in the regulatory agencies, so Chiang moved Sellers and the lab to his hometown, Alor Setar, in the northwest corner of peninsular Malaysia. It was pretty easy for him and Sellers to carry on in the same way in fact—they began to exaggerate costs and skim even more cash, which was channeled directly to Lung's terrorist group, CLAAC."

"I've never heard of this group before," Bolan said. "Should I have?"

"Kao Lung heads the group—of course, its real name is in Mandarin and I can't pronounce it. But Hank Chiang refers to it in English as China Liberated At All Costs—CLAAC. It's a radical group that started peacefully enough, but after the massacre at Tiananmen Square, they started finding justification for bloodshed. Lung was imprisoned and came out a little crazed, our sources say. He took over the group and turned it into a kind of Chinese IRA, whose agenda is the extermination of the upper-echelon hard-line Communists of the People's Republic—the old-timers dating from the early days, the ones CLAAC feels represent the worst impediment to rapid change.

"Lately Lung's started getting more impatient. He's angry at the U.S. for continuing its good relations with the Chinese government and for its bestowing most-favored-nation trade status on China. He wants the U.S. and the UN to provide aid in the violent overthrow of the Communists so that a democratic Chinese government—that's the rhetoric anyway—can be established.

"Lung's getting more and more obsessed with power. His followers are becoming increasingly obsessed with his ideology, and he's positioning himself to become a dictator."

Bolan had known the moment he looked at the photo that he was seeing a man in love with power, and a man of overwhelming arrogance. All that needed to be added to the mix was a touch of genius, and there'd be a despot in the making.

"I still don't see what the plan is or why we're involved."

"Lung's come up with a few ideas for humiliating the Communists and increasing global impatience with the slow pace of democratization in China," the big Fed said, exhaling as if he were very tired. "It involves Chinese nuclear reactors, many built from old Soviet blueprints—not quite up to Western safety specifications, easy to sabotage—and a sympathetic U.S. supporter with access to nuclear expertise."

Bolan felt a chill run through him. Now he knew why Brognola was so concerned. "Is Lung crazy enough to pull something like that?"

The big Fed leaned forward, elbows on his knees. "He's a damned Chinese Hitler with a major debt he feels he owes the Communists. Chiang believes in the sovereignty of China, or some such crap. He'll go for it. The key unknown is Sellers. He hasn't exactly had a history of demonstrating high regard for human life. Whether that means he'll cooperate in the murder of thousands or even tens of thousands..." Brognola shrugged. "But he's gone. Sellers has disappeared. We needed Chiang—we still need Chiang—to find Sellers and Lung."

"What makes you think Chiang would have talked if I'd nabbed him? He didn't seem too willing."

"He's built a cozy little life for himself. If we can get to him and give him a detailed description of the dismantling that's about to take place—of his business, his possessions, his family—I think he'll talk. Chiang is more important to Chiang than anything else, even the future of his motherland. He would rather not get involved in any of the messy details, either. He'd prefer to play at God—sit over here in his million-dollar home and call the shots on the liberation of China without getting his own hands dirty."

"I get the picture. What's CLAAC's target?"

"We don't know. There are a number of reactors in China, small and large, for energy production and other purposes.

"We're in fresh on this one. In fact, an operative more or less stumbled over the details while investigating the whereabouts of Sellers in connection with cancer cases starting to pop up in the vicinity of his Alor Setar lab. That's what got us interested. We were able to unearth the rest via a few well-placed taps. Our CIA friends provided the details on the People's Republic hit you foiled tonight.''

Bolan mulled the details. The situation kept getting stickier and stickier. ''The objective is clear-cut. Take out Lung. Foil the plan before it can get started. Where's Lung now if not in China?''

''We can't be sure. Sellers and Lung—hell, most of CLAAC's generals—are missing. We think Malaysia, protected by Chiang. He's still got government connections there, and enough cash to buy some serious privacy.''

''Then I've got to track down Chiang.''

Brognola shook his head. ''He's out of the country. EastStar's corporate jet left Meigs field in downtown Chicago thirty minutes after you called me—he must have driven directly there after your run-in with him at headquarters. We believe he's headed to Malaysia, too. Hopefully he's got himself and Lung holed up in the area of Alor Setar.''

Bolan nodded. ''And I'm going to Alor Setar after him.''

''That's up to you.'' The big Fed pushed a plane ticket across the table.

A SLATE GRAY CHEVROLET Suburban with dark windows was waiting for Mack Bolan at the tiny airport in Alor Setar, Malaysia. A young man in a starched white shirt and conservative maroon necktie was at the wheel.

''Good evening, sir, need a lift?''

''Yes. To a good restaurant.''

''How about Chinese food? Alor Setar has some of the best Chinese restaurants in Malaysia.''

Satisfied with the response, Bolan got into the vehicle. The young man pulled away instantly.

''Chen Tian, Mr. Belasko. You want to go to the hotel first?''

Tian was one of the CIA operatives Brognola had told him to expect to work with in Alor Setar—young but competent, the big Fed said. Bolan hadn't wasted any time taking this assignment. The image of nuclear sabotage in China had been deeply disturbing.

"The old EastStar labs are around here?"

"About twenty miles north. We think they're all but abandoned now."

"It's all we have to go on. Let's go there now."

"Right," Tian stated. "We thought you'd want to get started. We'll pick up Cello Jiahua and some hardware."

The Suburban veered off the road into a spotless neighborhood of compact dwellings and twisted through a disorienting series of turns. Tian halted before a yardless structure indistinguishable among the row of houses crowding against it. A porch light was on, and a small, slim figure dressed in black emerged with two large duffels, which were tossed in the back.

"Good evening." The woman who slid into the rear seat was Oriental, probably Chinese. She held out a hand. "Xiaoliao Jiahua. Call me Cello, like the musical instrument."

Taking her hand and introducing himself as Mike Belasko, the soldier wasn't surprised to find her grip strong. He'd known women like Jiahua—small, attractive, non-threatening in appearance. But underneath lay the strength and capabilities of years of training. She was undeniably attractive, even in the darkness of the Malaysian evening, with a soft mouth, short dark hair and glimmering green eyes.

"Tell me about the EastStar lab," Bolan said.

"EastStar more or less started here in Malaysia—Hank Chiang grew up in Alor Setar and started a company here in town, then took it to the U.S., where it really grew. A couple of years ago EastStar opened a new lab here and started doing a substantial amount of purification work,'' Jiahua explained. "They've also got a country club nearby. EastStar financed it and uses it as a vacation spot for their upper echelon and for living quarters for the execs while on business in the Alor Setar area.

"The laboratory used to have a lot of American staff. They were purifying and concentrating low-grade radioactive materials to be sold to U.S. companies, which use them for medical purposes. They had a lot of locals employed before they closed shop suddenly last month."

"Lots of people from Alor Setar lost jobs," Tian added. "Some have been getting sick since working at the labs."

"So what goes on in the facility now?"

"Nothing we know of. Maybe Hank Chiang has plans for it."

"Have you been inside?"

Tian grimaced. "We wanted to take a look yesterday but were ordered not to. I suppose we're too low on the totem pole to see what's inside. Whatever EastStar is up to must be pretty high-level activity in Washington's eyes."

Bolan nodded. Unbidden images had been coming to mind, specifically the horror that would result if Chiang and Kao Lung succeeded in their plan to sabotage a Chinese nuclear reactor. It had the potential to be another Chernobyl, or worse. Hundreds could die quickly, while thousands more could get doses of radiation severe enough to cause various cancers. What if CLAAC targeted a reactor near any sizeable city in the most populated country in the world, such as the new Daya Bay nuclear station near Hong Kong? How many millions would be dangerously exposed? How many would die?

KAO LUNG DRUMMED his fingers on the table in the dingy room above the activity of the streets of the Malaysian city of Sungai Petani. Across from him, Hang Chiang mopped his forehead with a grayish, balled handkerchief and then attempted, futilely, to fan himself with it. Lung thought he looked the perfect idiot.

Lung despised few human beings more than Hang Chiang. He hated the fact that the man was an American and had adopted American attitudes and life-style. He deplored Chiang's use of a Western nickname, and he was disgusted by Chiang's cowardice, for only a coward would hire men to fight his battles for him. But what Lung hated more than anything else was the fact that he was dependent on the man.

Chiang had contacted the group when it was still in its infancy and offered it funds and resources, and CLAAC had come to depend on these funds. Even freedom fighters needed sponsors. Even warriors for a new China needed to eat. Lung admitted that he was among those who became used to—addicted to—the type of freedom Chiang's contributions provided. Without the need to work, the group members could concentrate on their goals.

But Chiang was also from the United States, the nation that betrayed the people of China. By maintaining its relations with the murderous regime of hardline Communists that had killed so many peaceful demonstrators in Tiananmen Square, the U.S. revealed its true nature and its genuine motivation: its own welfare. The U.S. didn't concern itself with how one billion souls suffered under the oppressive yolk of communism, as long as it benefited. Through the exploitation of the poverty-level labor rates in the People's Republic, the United States of America profited substantially. Lung couldn't help but associate the manipulative capitalist Hang Chiang with the specter of the U.S. government. Despite his stated intentions, despite the contributions he made toward freeing China from the communists, Chiang was a symbol of America and its manipulative ways.

For Lung knew Chiang's true motivation—to become a leader of the new and reforged China, to gain power over the people he said he wanted freed.

This duplicity infuriated Lung. Somehow he'd managed to hide his anger so far.

"Who do you think this man was?"

Chiang laughed and waved his cigarette. "I have no idea. At first I thought you sent him. Then I realized you wouldn't have sent an American to protect me. That's when I decided to dump him, get him out of my hair."

"You think he's dead, then?"

"There's little chance he could have escaped. There must have been four or five Chinese guns shooting at him."

"Why are you convinced he was alone?" Lung asked.

"He was the only one I saw."

"If he came in after you, he knew the People's Republic was going to try to make the hit. If he knew the hit was about to go down, he probably knew how many men the PRC was sending. If so, why would he go in alone?"

Chiang's face was blank while he considered this. "I suppose he wouldn't."

"So there's no reason to suppose he didn't have backup—maybe they were already in a firefight with the Chinese and you simply failed to notice them. Obviously they would have been behind cover, and you were in quite a hurry to leave."

"I sure the hell was!" Chiang stated, then laughed. "I guess you're right, Kao. But what difference does it make?"

Chiang's foolish laughter had to be added to the list of hated features. He was always laughing and smiling, as if everything were a joke, including the fact that he had nearly been gunned down by Chinese agents. Also, he had been saved by an unknown American gunman, which meant some other agency, identity unknown but undoubtedly U.S., knew something about Chiang's involvement. This gunman even knew about CLAAC and had demanded information on its base of operations.

"It could make a world of difference if he was FBI or CIA. If they knew about an attempted hit even *you* were unaware of, then who knows what the extent of their information is? And to what degree they will further their involvement."

"I see." For once Chiang wasn't smiling. "What can we do?"

"Obviously there is nothing we can do." Lung didn't express any of the aggravation he felt. "We know nothing about this man. Since you left him behind, we have no clues as to his identity or where he was getting his information or what he planned to use his information to accomplish. Perhaps dumping him when you did was not the best course of action."

"Now you tell me." Chiang grinned sheepishly.

Lung's fist itched. He had to restrain himself from smashing that idiot smile from Chiang's face. Instead, he rose from the table, crossed to the bar and poured drinks for them both. He added a substantial amount of water to his own touch of vodka, almost none to Chiang's full glass of liquor, so that it looked as if they had equal drinks.

Lung sat at the heavy wooden table again, willing himself to adopt a relaxed manner. "You're right, Hang, there's nothing to do about it now. So we will do nothing."

"What if they come after us?"

"I doubt they can know where we are. You didn't tell him. Who have you told?"

Chiang considered this. "No one knows our location. Not even my wife. Unless we have a leak."

"A leak?" Lung downed a large gulp of his weak mixture. Chiang, like a monkey, imitated him, only his drink was much stronger and he swallowed it with some effort.

"A leak," Lung repeated. "There would be none among my men, of course. They are all loyal to the group." He paused, his eyes leveled calmly on Chiang's.

"Of course."

Lung wondered for the thousandth time how this idiot had become successful in the Western business world. "That leaves our Malaysian employees."

"Che Hing recommended each based on his ability to fire a gun and keep his mouth shut."

"How far can we trust even Che Hing? And how well can he know each and every man he's recommended? There is also your friend Steven Sellers."

"Sellers? He wouldn't risk his job security."

"Wrong. He'd risk anything and everything for more cash. The man cares about nothing except himself."

"He has been with me for over ten years."

"Loyalty is without importance to a man like him. I repeat—he cares only about himself. I have no doubts that he would betray you and the organization instantly for the right price."

Chiang gulped his vodka again without inducement. He was getting drunk, and when he was drunk he was easier for Lung to control. "I suppose you're right. But how can we find out if he's talked? And even if he has, we can't very well get rid of him. We need his expertise."

Lung shook his head. "Not anymore. I've found another expert whose services we can purchase."

Again Lung leveled his gaze at Chiang. The man was about to protest. Their agreement, forged years ago, was that they would have equal authority in the group. Outsiders wouldn't be brought in without the approval of both.

But Chiang was feeling chastized and weakened. He nodded. "Good. Good," he muttered. "Then let's lock up Sellers and make sure he gets out no more information—if he is our leak. Eventually we'll have to dispose of him anyway."

Lung considered this. Chiang was correct—Sellers should be isolated. And eventually eliminated.

But that had been the plan all along.

3

The Suburban was darkened, and Tian allowed it to roll to a stop at the base of the rocky hillside. Jiahua rummaged in one of the duffel bags, then handed Bolan a radio.

"I'll circle around to the front of this mountain after I leave you," Tian said. "That will get this wall of rock out from between us, and we should be able to communicate using these. But right here's the easiest access point if you don't want to be seen."

Bolan added the radio to his pack and stepped out of the vehicle.

"Come on," Jiahua said, quietly shutting the back door of the vehicle as she flung her own pack over one shoulder and started up the rough rock hill. Bolan followed and found the hill to be lit well enough by the clear night sky that he could see where he was going. The footholds were easy, and he lost no time climbing up the wall. His companion kept pace, and when they reached the top, they gazed directly out at the EastStar compound, a mile away over the flat, grassy ground.

Jiahua exchanged a wave with Tian, who started the Suburban and let the truck drift slowly and almost noiselessly around the corner of the hill, then was gone.

They started across the wide, open expanse of Malaysian grassland, and Bolan felt exposed under the clear, starlit sky.

He took them through the low, dark shadows of the shrub-like, grassy brush as much as possible.

"Watch out for snakes," Jiahua advised.

The soldier withdrew field glasses from his pack and peered through them at the darkened laboratory, seeing nothing that alarmed him: a simple boxy building surrounded by a nine-foot chain-link fence topped with barbed wire, an empty parking lot, a pale light illuminating the front of the building.

"I don't see signs of a security guard."

Jiahua squinted to try to see what Bolan was seeing without the aid of binoculars. "They used to keep one."

"If he's in there now, he's sitting in the dark."

They stayed low and crawled the last twenty feet to the fence on the west side of the building, where there was only a single window.

"Electrified?" Bolan asked in a whisper.

"No."

He stared at the gray metal chain of the fence for a moment.

"It's not." The woman reached for it as a demonstration, gasping slightly when Bolan grabbed her wrist. He nodded at the rotting remnants of a small hare lying next to the fence.

"Let's just be certain," he suggested, rummaging in his pack briefly. He found rubber-handled wire cutters and struck at the fence with them. The sparks were blue and crackled.

"Shit," Jiahua whispered.

Bolan applied the cutters to the fence, which was heavy-gauge metal, so the going was slow. The smoke from the sparks was plainly visible. In a few minutes he had cut a circle out of the fence the size of a manhole cover and had ruined the cutters. He dropped to all fours and crawled through quickly, guiding his companion when she followed him.

"See that back door?" she said. "I think we can get in there."

They circled cautiously, staying close to the fence and as deep in the grass as possible. There was no light illuminating the back of the building, and there were just a couple of windows. From their position Bolan could see a low dip in the rock, through which glimmered the distant lights of the town of Alor Setar, several miles away.

"Any alarm system?" he asked.

"Not that I'm aware of."

They made a quick run through the open grassland into the darkness of the building's shadow. Pressing himself against the building door, Bolan listened for sound and felt for vibration, any sign of someone inside the place. There was nothing. He picked the lock easily and swung open the steel fire door just enough for him and Jiahua to slip inside.

The laboratory was completely dark. Their flashlights picked out piles of trashed equipment. A dusty robotic arm dangled limply from the ceiling inside a huge glass case; a door in the case was wide open. Glass containers were scattered inside the enclosure.

Bolan heard a clicking sound and found Jiahua peering anxiously at the readout of a tiny instrument, which she waved in the direction of the glass case. It was a Geiger counter, measuring microrads.

"Is this place hot?"

"Warm, more like it. There are faint traces of radiation from the case and a little more in the corner—nothing dangerous or out of the ordinary for a safely run radiation laboratory after the radioactive material has been gone for a few months."

"Which would be about right if they moved the material when they supposedly ceased operations here—EastStar's legitimate operations, anyway. Let's see what else we can find."

"It would help if I had more of a clue as to what you're looking for, Mr. Belasko."

"Ideally some clue as to Hank Chiang's real base of operations. We believe it's here in Malaysia."

Jiahua shrugged at the brevity of the explanation. That was some information to go on, at least. This Belasko character wasn't exactly forthcoming with data, but he exuded an air of confidence and, well, she wanted to call it *experience,* as if he were a man used to being in life-threatening situations.

She determined to focus on the job at hand—find some clue as to Chiang's Malaysian headquarters. She opened a desk drawer, found it half-full of trashed technical files and closed it. Threading between dusty lab tables, carelessly left equipment, dropped trash and discarded paraphernalia, she made her way to the front of the large lab. She tried a door, peered through it carefully, then entered a tiny, windowless office. She found another file drawer and riffled through its contents—useless purification reports on low-rad barium compounds—and froze.

It took her a full five seconds to identify the sound she was hearing, but only a fraction of a second passed after that before she had stormed back into the lab, drawing her Colt 2000 DA Auto 9 mm handgun. Bolan had already realized something was amiss.

"That's a chopper, coming from the city."

"EastStar owns one and keeps it at their other facility," Jiahua stated.

"I thought you said that facility was a vacation condo."

"Well, it's a big vacation condo. They have several buildings, rooms for forty, golf course, the works."

"I wish you'd told me about that before. Sounds like what we're looking for."

"Can't be," she protested. "It's a damned country club."

"We don't have time to discuss it now. Come on." He headed toward the back entrance, the Desert Eagle filling his hand. He stopped at the door just long enough to get an audible bearing on the helicopter; it hadn't yet passed over the top of the building from the front. He slammed through the door, Jiahua on his heels, closing the door quickly, pressing back against the wall of the building. They were in the shadow for the moment. If the chopper was equipped with a searchlight, they would be instantly targeted.

"What'll we do now?" the CIA agent asked.

Bolan sensed the twinge of desperation in her voice. The truth was he had no idea what to do next. There was no hiding place they would reach undetected if the chopper had lights, except for the building itself, and staying inside might be suicide. The roar of the approaching helicopter told them it was on top of the building, and then it screamed out over the grassland in front of them, lights blazing like a UFO, and began its turn.

"This way," Bolan commanded, and they ran around the side of the building, out of sight of the chopper. But the soldier knew they could easily have been spotted anyway. They waited to hear what the chopper's occupants would do, and listened as the aircraft landed inside the perimeter fence.

"They must have had the fence wired with an alarm," Jiahua suggested nervously.

"Maybe," Bolan answered. But he doubted it.

"Or the building."

"That's more likely. It's irrelevant now."

The Executioner stepped to the corner and peered at the activity around the helicopter as it disgorged five men. All were armed with assault rifles and were shouting among themselves in what sounded like Bahasa Malay, the most commonly used language of the country. The group raced toward the building and burst through the back door while the chopper's rotors accelerated to a whine and the craft took to the air to patrol the grounds from above. The aircraft swooped in a huge circle over the grassland and headed in their direction, two blazing searchlights illuminating vast swathes of landscape. Bolan and Jiahua would find themselves a part of that landscape in seconds.

They sprinted to the front of the building, sliding around the corner just a few feet ahead of the light that would reveal them to the chopper pilot. Bolan raised the Desert Eagle and aimed carefully at the helicopter as it roared into view again to sweep the front of the structure with its lights. But the Desert Eagle tracked the chopper carefully, then spit out three rounds.

"Did you get him?"

Bolan didn't answer, but the helicopter began to shudder as if out of control. It hovered twenty feet above the ground for a moment, then plummeted, landing with a crunch of metal that crushed its landing gear and crumpled the metal belly. The rotors were still spinning, but the pilot was a mass of blood behind the controls. He slumped forward suddenly and was still.

The front door of the building burst open, and the first hardman didn't even see the Executioner until it was too late. Bolan shot the rifle out of his grip and took off most of his hands. The man dropped to the earth, screaming. Bolan quickly observed that the fallen gun was a Chinese Type 56, the PRC's imitation of an AK 47.

The door slammed shut behind him before the others emerged. The EastStar hardmen knew now where he was. Bolan barked an order to his companion, and they raced again to the back of the building.

The back door was quiet. None of the four remaining gunners was attempting to get out that way, but there was a tinkle of glass in the distance. Bolan ran along the back of the building, ducking under the windows, to the back corner on the western side. A hardman raced in his direction, while another was extricating himself from the window. The gunner raised his rifle to fire from the hip but learned the disadvantage of the weapon in such a situation—it was impossible for him to react as fast as the man who held the Desert Eagle. A bullet drilled through his heart before he could touch the rifle's trigger.

The man in the window was desperately trying to bring his own rifle into play and found it impossible. He screamed in Malay, probably trying to persuade the others inside to pull him back in. But it was too late. Bolan homed in on him and fired again. The man flopped against the window frame, then rolled limply to the ground.

Three of the five were downed. A blast of gunfire erupted from the window. It was panic fire, without hope of actually getting Bolan—the soldier knew from the rate of fire that the man responsible was losing his cool. The gunfire halted and the night was silent.

Jiahua had put away her Colt handgun and extracted a tool with a little more stopping power from her pack. A Heckler & Koch MP-5 A-5 submachine gun was nestled comfortably in her grip. She was waiting patiently, but her eyes were blazing with excitement.

"You go to the front," Bolan said in the same moment his next strategy formed itself. "Fire at the front door and windows. I'll wait back here and pick them off when they try to get out.''

''What if they try to come out the front anyway?''

''Don't stop shooting.''

The woman nodded and breathed deep, then sprinted to the front of the building, leaping the corpses and ducking the window. Bolan didn't have time to worry about her. She was CIA, which intimated she'd probably been in tough situations before. He hoped she didn't freeze. She reached the edge of the wall and began to fire around the corner. Bolan heard the explosive shattering of glass as she took out the front windows.

He waited while the two hardmen inside weighed their options, took stock of the situation. Bolan was counting on the probability that they didn't realize there were two assailants outside the building. If they guessed wrong, they would surely take another exit. That didn't necessarily make the back door the most likely egress....

His ears caught the distant sound of tinkling glass. Jiahua paused in her firing at that moment, and the timing was opportune—the breaking-glass sound came from the eastern side of the building.

Bolan bolted around the back of the building, ducking under the first window, but he hadn't counted on the windows in the back door. There was a blast of fire as he raced past, and he jerked sideways. Heavy rounds drilled through the air inches from his body. He twisted in a complete circle and fired directly into the door. The Desert Eagle punched fist-sized holes in the wood, and he heard the sound of a rifle clattering to the floor. He checked around the eastern corner—the hardman had exited through the window and was running toward the front of the building, already rounding the corner.

The Executioner whipped the Desert Eagle into firing position without much hope of getting the fleeing gunner, then heard the distant sound of 9 mm gunfire. The enemy jerked on his feet as the bullets impacted his body, then slumped to the dry earth. Jiahua stepped from behind the building and nudged the body with a look of distaste.

Bolan gestured for her to join him, and they crept quietly, low to the ground, to the laboratory's back door. There was silence behind it. Bolan signaled for Jiahua to pull the door open. She did so, and the soldier stepped inside, Desert Eagle leveled.

The man Bolan had shot through the door was just inside, his legs wrapped uncomfortably beneath him. By his side was a large F-88, an Australian version of the 5.56 mm Steyr AUG rifle with a transparent plastic magazine.

He was the fifth and final hardman.

Jiahua grinned and sighed in relief. "That was pretty hairy."

"Raise Chen on the radio. We'd better get out of here before they send reinforcements."

"Right."

They left the building and walked around to the front. By then Jiahua was worried.

"He's not answering," she said, pointing to her radio.

"I'll try," Bolan took his own radio from his pack. He clicked it on and spoke the code word his companion had just used. Static was the only reply.

"Shit. They've got him."

"You may be right." Bolan approached the idling helicopter. It was a Hughes Model 500D, with room for a pilot plus six crew and a cruising speed of about 160 mph. "It still looks operational," he commented. "You said the EastStar housing compound is nearby. I assume it's well guarded."

"Yeah. Very well guarded. Security system and more fences and all that stuff. We have no idea how many staff or residents are there right now."

"But we can assume the chopper came from there?"

"It must have. They may have a bigger operation there than Chen and I ever suspected. That means it's going to be a real bitch to infiltrate."

"This may better our chances," Bolan said.

The soldier jumped into the mangled chopper and wrestled the corpse out of the pilot's seat, pushing him into the rear. He tested the speed control, and the rotors responded with increased pitch.

"Ever flown a helicopter?" Jiahua asked, sliding into the passenger seat.

"Once or twice."

There was a grinding sensation from the release of pressure on the crushed underbelly of the machine, which could be felt in the frame of the chopper, as well as heard. The ground fell gradually away from them, and they hovered at fifteen feet for a few seconds to ensure that the craft was capable of remaining airborne.

It took them less than ten minutes to sight the EastStar housing compound. From their traveling altitude of under thirty feet, Bolan saw only a very tall wooden security wall and the tops of some three-story structures inside. Floodlights were in place to make a nighttime approach.

"What's inside?"

"One building is a hotel with twenty rooms or so. Another building houses meeting rooms and a restaurant. A third is a recreational facility—you know, gym and pool and stuff. Beyond that is a nine-hole golf course and a soccer field, a few smaller-maintenance type buildings and staff housing."

"Sounds like a resort."

"It is a resort. Or else it was until a couple of months ago. EastStar always has execs from the U.S. and Pacific Rim coming in."

"Sounds like it would be a perfect place to hide a small army, too," Bolan commented. "Duck. We're going in."

The helicopter roared over the fence with a surge of speed, halting in midair, then zooming forward again. Jiahua stayed low on the front bench seat. Bolan sent the aircraft in a 360-degree spin while he made a mental photograph of the compound below him and searched for the expanse of the golf course. Figures were already rushing out of buildings below, seeing that their chopper was badly smashed and apparently barely under control.

He spotted a likely patch of green a few hundred yards distant, unlit and empty. He flooded more fuel into the engine and sent the aircraft careering at top speed in the direction of the green, staying less than a dozen feet from the ground, then stopping suddenly and lowering the machine to the earth. It smashed to the ground, and the engine choked, nearly stalling. Bolan killed the lights.

"Get out," he said quickly. "Get to the trees."

"What are you going to do?"

"I'll be right behind you."

Jiahua fled into the darkness. Bolan hoisted the dead pilot out of the seat behind them and put him in the pilot's seat, watching the erratic beams of approaching flashlights. He dived from the ruined craft and sprinted into the trees, keeping the chopper between himself and the group from the compound. He and Jiahua crouched in the well-manicured shrubbery at the edge of the green and watched the group swarm the helicopter. The dead pilot was pulled out and left to lie unceremoniously on the fairway.

The chopper's ignition was turned off, and the rotors spun to a halt. Bolan heard the men speak in angry tones, then they hurried back to the compound. Shortly thereafter, several vehicles started and headed out.

"They're going back to the laboratory to see if we were foolish enough to stick around," Bolan said. "Let's go find Chen."

They clung to the shadowy edge of the artificial forest on the golf course until it led them to a maintenance building. The hotel area was probably well lit under normal circumstances, but in its current alert status, all the compound's exterior lights were blazing. The Executioner knew they were in imminent danger of being spotted. The only saving grace was the fact that many, maybe most, of the troops stationed here were out looking for them elsewhere.

He scoped out the area from behind the maintenance building, then led Jiahua across the open into the somewhat enclosed area under an exterior stairwell. As they made the run, he glimpsed the gray Suburban.

"Did you see that?" his companion asked as they crouched in the shadows. "They do have Chen."

"We knew that."

"I was holding out some hope that he'd escaped."

"He still might have." But Bolan had his doubts.

He led the way around the back of the hotel, halting under each ground-floor window, several of which were lit, listening for any clue that might indicate Tian was being held inside. There was nothing to hear.

By the time they reached the last window, Bolan heard the sound of vehicles returning to the compound. It hadn't taken long for them to reach the laboratory and find the remains of their comrades. Someone roared something in Chinese-accented Malay as the first vehicle could be heard stopping. Then the Malay faltered and changed to English.

"Where the hell is Che Hing?"

"Right here, boss."

"Your 'elite squad' has been neutralized. What do you have to say for yourself?"

"Those were some of the best men I've ever worked with."

"Not good enough! They're all dead, every one of them. And they didn't even manage to kill their assailants in the process. This is the best you have to offer?"

"My apologies, Captain Ming, but surely—"

"Apology not accepted. If you can't do better than that, then we have no business to transact together. Do you understand? Now, whoever it was is still out there because your men failed to stop them! If it wasn't for my men spotting their vehicle, they would have escaped free and clear by this time. As it is, they are still on foot. We can assume they are still in the grasslands trying to reach Alor Setar by dawn. I want you to get out there and find them by sunup. Understood?"

There was some mumbling of further apology, then Bolan heard the Malaysian yelling orders. There were further sounds of vehicles leaving the scene.

They waited in the shadows for half an hour, by which time the compound had grown quieter. Occasionally a sentry would pass by. Bolan could only assume that the CLAAC captain, Ming, would be trying to pry more information out of Chen Tian.

He ordered Jiahua to return to the comparative isolation and safety of the maintenance shack, then crept out of their spot behind the hotel, taking temporary cover behind a large air-conditioning unit. Bolan watched as another Malaysian guard hurried to the one-story office structure. He was about to knock when the door opened and a gaunt Chinese man with bruised-looking eyes emerged.

"Report!"

"Che Hing has called in. He says that he has all his men in the area around the laboratory. He says he can find no sign of them at this time."

"No sign! They can't have disappeared. We have their getaway vehicle."

"Perhaps they had another," the guard suggested.

"Not likely. Tell Che Hing to keep looking. In fact, tell him not to come back without them."

"Yes."

Bolan watched Ming close the door carefully behind him. As he and the guard entered another building, the Executioner scanned for sentries. There would be one or more, he was certain. Atop the hotel, almost out of his range of vision, he located a small, open-air post. A sentry would be stationed there, but Bolan couldn't spot him from his vantage point.

Adjusting the Beretta's fire selector to 3-round-burst mode, Bolan stepped from behind the air conditioner and walked forward calmly, in plain sight. He knew the guard saw him and might even have tentatively identified him as a stranger. But the soldier's straightforward behavior created enough doubt in the guard's mind that he didn't yet sound the alarm.

Bolan reached the far side of the courtyard, turned quickly to face the guard—who was staring at him intently from the housetop post—and pulled the trigger on the Beretta. The first two bullets pierced the guard's sternum in the very instant he had decided he had better sound the alarm. The third pierced his jaw before he had a chance to scream. He was dead before his limp torso draped over the low wall.

The Executioner stepped quickly to the door of the building Ming had recently left and slipped inside, the Beretta leading the way. But he found himself in a silent, darkened room with a desk, a single reading lamp and a file

cabinet. The desk and cabinet top were bare. He moved on
into a hall, which was almost pitch-black, and stood in the
darkness for a long moment before his vision adjusted well
enough for him to find his way. At the end of the corridor
was another door, which opened into a small theater. It
contained no more than thirty red-velvet seats. Heavy red
curtains were pulled back from the stage, revealing the
backdrop—a massive EastStar logo. Illuminated by the
footlights was Chen Tian, bloody and bound to a chair. A
guard sat in the front row, an Uzi submachine gun on his
lap.

Bolan stepped quietly down the well-carpeted aisle and
approached the guard from the rear, placing the Beretta
against the guard's skull.

"Don't even twitch."

"Who are you?" the man asked in heavily accented English.

"Where are Hank Chiang and Kao Lung?"

"You think I am some fool to answer your questions?"

Bolan stepped out from behind the man and walked up
onto the stage, the Beretta never wavering from the Chinese guard. He felt Tian's wrist quickly and found a feeble
pulse.

"Who is it?" the CIA man asked, raising his head. His
eyes were bloody and swollen shut.

"Belasko."

"You have got to get out of here, Belasko. Chiang and
Lung aren't here. They're in Sungai Petani. I heard Ming
discussing it. They're at a place called Adro Alloy."

The guard acted suddenly, grabbing the machine gun
from his lap. Bolan fired, and the three rounds drilled into
the man's shoulder and chest. He bent forward, groaning,
but he managed to squeeze off a short burst before another

triburst took him out. But the guard's autofire had slapped into Tian, killing him.

There were shouts from outside. The machine-gun fire hadn't gone unnoticed. Bolan exited stage right and found another hallway, which led to a back door. Suddenly he was outside again but exposed in the bright compound lights. He sprinted across a stretch of grass.

"Halt!"

The Executioner twisted sideways and fired at the source of the command, and a short Malaysian with a rifle clutched his chest and collapsed to the ground. Bolan sprinted around the building and found himself in the courtyard. Two guards were racing across the compound and spotted him immediately. They weren't prepared, and they weren't fast enough. The Beretta spit lead, and they fell instantly.

The brick pavement shattered just to the soldier's right, and the retort of a large-calibre handgun echoed through the buildings. Bolan traced the shot to a second-story window in the house—it was the CLAAC captain, Ming, leaning out with a large-barreled handgun. Bolan dodged the second shot and fired at the window. He heard a scream of frustration followed by a shout in Mandarin.

More footsteps were approaching, and Bolan holstered the Beretta in favor of the more powerful Desert Eagle. He waited a fraction of a second, then fired at the far end of the house as more guards stormed into the courtyard. The leader took the .44 Magnum round full in the abdomen, and his collapsing body tripped up his surprised comrades. Meanwhile, the soldier spotted movement to his left. A tiny, black-clad figure materialized from the other side of the hotel and slipped behind the wheel of Chen Tian's Suburban. The engine rushed to life and, at high revs, Jiahua dropped the transmission into reverse. Bolan was sending round after round at the group of guards, who had yet to recover their wits. They regrouped as the Suburban spun in a backward half circle and screeched to a halt inches from the big American. He yanked the door open and jumped inside, then fired again, one arm out the passenger window. Two more guards toppled, but several shots were fired, twice penetrating the windshield near the top.

The Suburban accelerated quickly in the direction of the fence, and Bolan half climbed out his window as they neared the gate. A pair of Malay guards waited for them, and the quicker of the two aimed his assault rifle at Jiahua. Bolan fired instantly, and the guard was never able to get off his shot. The Executioner's second round knocked the remaining guard off his feet, his machine gun clattering on the pavement.

Bolan pulled himself back inside just as Jiahua slammed the front end of the Suburban into the heavy wooden gate. The sound of collapsing metal and crunching wood was tremendous, but the mass of the vehicle carried it through. It bounced over the incline onto the road and headed for the town of Alor Setar at ninety miles per hour.

4

Forty miles south, in the city of Sungai Petani, Hank Chiang rested his elbows on his knees, staring at the floor of the old plant. Kao Lung slammed down the phone.

"Your friend struck again, Hang Chiang."

"We don't know it was him for sure."

"It was him. And, as I guessed, he has help. Our sources say the driver we captured and killed might very well be CIA."

Chiang paled, then plucked at the wrinkled mess of a shirt he had flung on ten minutes earlier when Lung sent one of his goons to pound on his door. It was three-thirty in the morning, and the news was very bad. The laboratory and compound in Alor Setar had been infiltrated. Losses were heavy.

"I've ordered them to move out immediately. They're stripping the lab. When they're done, they're going to dynamite it. The compound will be abandoned."

"Well, those were obvious targets. It was common knowledge that they were EastStar property. Once I had been identified, it was inevitable that they would target other EastStar locales I might make use of. We simply move everybody on to Ompang. That's not an EastStar facility. They'll never know to find our people there," Chiang said. "We'll be safe." He meant to sound reassuring. Instead, it sounded like a question.

"We will have to move there, as well," Lung said. "They may have found information on this facility. We can't take the chance of them tracking us here."

"Then I don't know how good an idea it is for us to move in with the rest of the operation."

Lung was silent, gazing at him calmly, as if he knew Chiang had more to say by way of explanation.

"We can monitor Ompang. Maybe set up a headquarters base in Kuantan. It's a big city. It would be easy for us to stay lost there should the rest of the operation be uncovered."

"You believe the operation may be brought down?"

Chiang grinned, and he shrugged. "Any venture has a chance of failure, however small. It's good advice to insulate oneself from failure that might occur while being in position to reap the benefits when it succeeds."

"That sounds like cowardice."

"It is good business practice."

Lung's fist hit the table. "This is not business. This is the humiliation of the totalitarian government of China."

"Kao, you included me in this venture because I believe in your ideals, in the dream of a China free of the yoke of communism. But also because I possess organizational skills that have allowed me to prosper in the free world. I know how to get things done. If you no longer want my advice, I will leave and allow you to organize your operation as you see fit."

Lung looked into Chiang's face and realized he had made an error of judgment. He couldn't easily humiliate the man into following his orders. Chiang had a sense of self-preservation and savvy that wouldn't allow his pride to leverage him into making what he considered to be poor judgment calls. And he still held the most important of all the cards—the finances that would pay for the completion of

he initial stage of the operation here in Malaysia and the
ransport of the operation to China, where the "Fire Ham-
ner" would fall. And then the world would notice. Then
:ao Lung would be famous. The government of the Peo-
·le's Republic would receive such a blow that it would never
ecover.

Lung could afford to put up with Chiang's cowardice and
elf-preservation instincts a while longer. Once the Ham-
ner fell, he would have offers of financing coming in from
ll over the world. He wouldn't need Chiang any longer.

"You are right Chiang. What do I know of organizing
uch a complicated venture? However, I simply cannot
ondone removing ourselves from the most important as-
·ects of the training taking place in Ompang. I must be
here. If you wish to remain in Kuantan, so be it."

Chiang thought a moment and nodded. "All right. We
oin the others in Ompang. With all of CLAAC in one
·lace. Anyway, I doubt anyone will have the balls to attack
s." Chiang chuckled when he thought of his nameless
American adversary trying to break into the compound he
nd Lung were constructing in Ompang.

"On that I agree. We'll move out by morning."

"Meanwhile, there's the matter of this facility. Let's not
imply abandon it. Let's make use of it."

Chiang began laying out his plan. It was the first of his
·lans that Lung actually approved of.

ADRO ALLOY HADN'T BEEN in business in about a decade by
he look of the warehouse. The massive building stood rot-
ing in the streets of Sungai Petani, along with the remains
·f several other failed ventures and a few that somehow re-
nained in business without being able to afford decent fa-
ilities. In the early morning the streets were already filling
vith low-wage workers and the vendors that catered to them

on a daily basis. No street-corner tourist stops here, full of brightly colored souvenirs and English-language periodicals. Instead, there were wooden shacks with flimsy, glossy Malay-language magazines, stands full of fruit getting hot in the morning sun, women marketing cheaply made clothing. Most of the workers were streaming toward a large soy processing plant on the opposite side of the street, and the air was full of the thick stench of fermenting bean curd. No one was entering or leaving the building marked Adro Alloy.

Mack Bolan stepped through the crowds with the calm air of one who could be at ease in a foreign city. His ease made him less conspicuous. Only a few Malaysians noticed that he was obviously not a Far Easterner. He traveled with the general flow of pedestrians until he was across from Adro Alloy, then cut across to an alley, stepping over an Indian woman and her child crouched at the alley entrance accepting donations. The door to the warehouse posed no problem, and the soldier entered the plant.

The plant was illuminated by the morning sun peeking in through filthy windows. The air was dank and torrid. He crept among the mounds of greasy hulks of unused equipment until he heard voices speaking Malay. He followed the sound up a flight of steel stairs to a second-floor office.

Two men were discussing a Thai television show, and they appeared to be hired guards, not CLAAC members. Bolan passed the office and proceeded into the heart of the plant. Here it was wide open, with more filthy windows allowing some morning sun to shine along the back wall. There were no Chinese. Obviously the men in the office were CLAAC employees, but Bolan seriously doubted they had any useful information. He'd come to a dead end.

Something moved in the hazy light, and Bolan dropped to the floor. It had been a barely perceptible shift, perhaps nothing at all. Then he heard muttering in Mandarin followed by the stuttering of a 9 mm Uzi. The bullets pounded off the walls and equipment, but Bolan had already sunk low behind a large worktable, below the line of fire. When the gunfire halted momentarily, he jumped up and fired in the direction of the gunman. The figure toppled in the darkness, but another flurry of fire erupted from two points. And now the Malaysians from the office were emerging to join the battle.

Bolan scanned the warehouse behind him. No exits. He now realized he had walked into a trap and was not terribly pleased with himself. Securing better cover behind a large stainless-steel chemical bath, he leaned around the corner and fired at the Malaysian gunners as they stormed down the stairs to join the Chinese. Three of them collapsed on the stairs, and the rest sprang for cover.

The Chinese had homed in on the chemical bath, and the old steel sink echoed with the impact of their fire. Bolan realized his assailants had the advantage of the windows—the sun was shining in from the glass above, making him a well-defined silhouette every time he came into view. No light was shining on his attackers.

The warehouse floor was littered with many pieces of old equipment. The soldier made careful use of it, moving across the warehouse from one side to the other, dodging from cover to cover until his attackers lost him. There were confused shouts in Mandarin, Malay and English. Gunfire from the far end played around the warehouse haphazardly.

Bolan found safe cover and assessed the situation. He was trapped, no way out except forward, and there were at least two Chinese and maybe a half-dozen Malaysian gunners waiting to bring him down. He couldn't see any of them in the bad light of the warehouse, and he couldn't shoot what he couldn't see.

A plan formed and he acted on it instantly. He found an AN-M14 grenade in his backpack, which had been among the arms Cello Jiahua had provided. He activated the bomb, held it for a moment—not counting, going on instinct—then jumped to his feet. He lobbed the grenade directly at the ceiling and dived back down again as a fresh flurry of gunfire flew toward his position. He rolled underneath a steel worktable as the air was blasted by the explosion of the grenade. Bolan was concerned it might have gone off just a fraction of a second early, but a rain of debris followed the blast—shattered wood, twisted metal, crumbled glass. He covered his face with his arm to protect himself from the debris as it bounced off the floor and heard the cries of alarm and confusion.

Suddenly the sun was shining in through the newly created hole in the ceiling, and the entire warehouse was brightly lit. The Executioner had clear targets. The Chinese and Malaysians were covered in debris, and several had been temporarily blinded by the falling glass and dust. The Desert Eagle took out those gunners still able to raise their weapons. The first to fall were the two Chinese, followed by two Malaysians.

A Chinese hardman appeared on the stair landing and leveled his gun at Bolan. The soldier reacted instinctively, and the Desert Eagle homed in—then he stopped. The gunman's arms had flopped to his sides, and his handgun clattered to the steel grid floor. Blood streamed from his mouth, and he collapsed.

Bolan ducked rifle fire from the floor and squeezed off another two rounds at the Malaysian gunning for him. The hardman decided to make a desperate run for it and headed for the stairs. He reached the top only to be flung into the open air by another gunshot fired by the same gunner who had downed the Chinese. There was a sudden silence.

A small, boyish Chinese man ran to the edge of the landing and faced Bolan over the distance of the warehouse, the Taurus PT 101 in his right hand held in readiness but pointed at the ceiling. The Desert Eagle was pointed directly at his chest from a distance no greater than fifteen yards. It was a sure killing shot.

"You are CIA?" the Chinese asked.

"Who are you?"

"Wai Bao, People's Republic of China secret service."

"Drop it!" It was Jiahua's voice, but Bolan couldn't see her. The agent's head twitched sideways, but he didn't look behind him. He raised his gun hand out to his side and let the Taurus fall to the steel-grate floor.

"That is CIA," Wai Bao said. "One can tell them by the way they shout."

"You've got some explaining to do. Belasko, you okay?"

"Yes," Bolan said. "How do we know you're really from the Chinese government?"

"No way to prove it to you now, and I would suggest we don't have the time to linger at the scene of the crime, eh?"

"You think we're going to trust you?" Jiahua asked.

"I have been tracking Kao Lung for two years, and I came with him from China. I have infiltrated CLAAC, and I am one of its most trusted members. You would be foolish to give up the opportunity of working with someone who already had so much inside information on this organization."

"He's right. We can't afford not to make use of his connection if he is telling the truth." Bolan flung his backpack to Jiahua, who caught it with a swipe at the air that didn't compromise the steady gun barrel held on her captive. "There's twine inside. Tie his hands."

''We don't have much time,'' Bao said levelly. ''I would suggest that the Sungai Petani police will not be so slow to respond to the kinds of noises that have been coming from this warehouse in the last five minutes. And I have a car.''

Bolan thought quickly, then he frisked Bao one-handed, swiftly determining the man was hiding no identification or weapons that might undermine the story he had told. He had to agree with the man—time, at the moment, was of the essence.

''All right. Let's go.'' He nodded toward the exit and gave his companion a hard look when she was about to protest.

The door closed behind them.

THE BLOOD-COVERED Chinese gunman who'd been shot by Wai Bao shuddered and flopped onto his stomach, the impact forcing a yelp from him. He reached out before him and meshed his fingers into the grate floor, dragging his body forward with his arms.

After progressing some ten feet across the floor, he paused to rest. His vision focused through the grate to the warehouse floor fifteen feet below, where a black liquid of some type was trickling down as if from a leaky pipe. He realized it was his own blood, seeping out of him and through the grate floor at a tremendous rate, splattering on the filthy warehouse floor. No human could live long while suffering blood loss that severe. He was motivated to greater effort.

A moment later he reached the office and managed to pull himself to a counter where the telephone sat. The effort required to grasp the cord was almost too much. The phone crashed to the floor.

When he saw that the phone was a rotary-dial model, he sobbed in frustration. He didn't know if he had the will or the strength to dial it, and his vision was clouding. But he did it, one interminable number at a time. When he finished dialing, he rested his head on the floor next to the receiver. He heard a voice in a car several miles away, the voice of Kao Lung.

The man tried to speak, but the sound emerged as a gasp.

"Who is this?"

"Wai Bao," the wounded man said in Mandarin just before the last wisp of strength seeped from his body, "betrayed..."

In a truck heading southeast through the outskirts of Sungai Petani, Kao Lung heard the rush of air filtering through the man's teeth as death claimed him.

5

Bolan heard the fax paper bearing Wai Bao's fingerprints rattling in Brognola's hand several thousand miles away in Washington, D.C.

"The man checks out. Our Intel confirms he's an agent for the PRC and he's been tracking CLAAC," the big Fed said. "Get this, though—he's been undercover with the group for almost three years. In fact, he's been there since the group started its transformation from a peaceful pro-democracy bunch to a quasiterrorist association."

"That's a long time to be undercover. How can we be sure he hasn't become sympathetic to the group?"

"You tell me. The PRC hasn't gone after him themselves. I suppose that means something. And you said he did shoot a couple of CLAAC members in cold blood."

"It was at the end of the firefight, and I was doing pretty well for myself. If he was so willing to help me out, how come he didn't start shooting long before that?"

"I thought he'd claimed to be out in his car."

"He did. It may be the truth."

"You aren't sure."

"No, I'm not. But I'm going to see what I can get out of him in terms of voluntary or involuntary cooperation. I'll be in touch."

Bolan hung up, crossed the massive lobby of the dank, decrepit hotel and made his way to Bao's room. He found

Jiahua in the seat under the window, her handgun on her lap, glaring at Wai Bao, who reclined on the bed, relaxed.

"My sources say you're for real."

Bao nodded. "Good. You must allow me to check in with Kao Lung right away. My cover is in danger."

"Go ahead."

LUNG WASN'T SURPRISED when he heard Bao's voice on the other end. "My friend, we heard the police reports and feared we'd lost you."

Bao was trying to catch his breath, by the sound of his voice. He explained about escaping just ahead of a group that stormed the Sungai Petani warehouse, shooting down everyone in sight. He had just barely made it to the car and escaped, but had been followed through the streets of Sungai Petani for over an hour before shaking the tail. "I think I'm safe now. But I'm afraid I may be the only one to have gotten out alive."

"Such is the case," Lung admitted. "But are you all right? You aren't wounded?"

"I'm just tired. I will be fine." Bao asked Lung where he should meet up with the rest of the group.

"You'll not be joining the rest of us yet. We are on our way out of the city now, and there is a job for you here. I had meant to tell Guo Le to do this thing. Now Guo Le is dead. You have become my new lieutenant."

Bao humbly expressed his gratitude at the promotion.

"So, Lieutenant, you have this task to perform. A new expert is being brought in from the United States—a scientist who will act as a consultant. He'll arrive in Sungai Petani from Los Angeles via Kuala Lumpur at 4:00 p.m. on Malay Air flight 105. Meet him at the airport. He'll give you driving instructions from there. A chauffeuring errand might not seem like an adequately important task for a

CLAAC lieutenant, but I assure you it is. Mr. Thomas Comas is an expert on reactor design. Only recently has he been convinced to become involved with CLAAC. He'll give us much more vital information than our current consultant. Our Mr. Sellers has become less useful than he once was."

Bao said he would meet Mr. Comas at the airport.

"I'm very pleased you, at least, are alive, my old friend," Lung said. "Be cautious. Be wary. I will see you tonight."

Wai Bao swore his loyalty, and the line went dead.

SITTING IN THE TRUCK, now parked at a service station some twenty miles outside Sungai Petani, Lung slowly placed the cellular phone on the dashboard.

Chiang walked across the parking lot from his own car to the window of the truck.

"Well?"

"Bao is bringing himself to us, as well as the rest of the vermin, I assume. We'll have a trap waiting for them."

"That's what you said before," Chiang complained.

Lung's eyes burned with anger that wasn't necessarily directed at Chiang. "Before I didn't know all the rats. Now I do."

THE SUNGAI PETANI AIRPORT main terminal was a vast cavern, the air hot and thick. At least two thousand people were within sight from Bolan's viewpoint, against a wall next to a cubicle selling liquor and tobacco products.

"Man, I don't like the smell of this." Cello Jiahua leaned against the wall next to him, gazing idly into the glass front of the tiny shop as if trying to select a vodka.

"Me, neither. But Bao is a lead to Chiang and the rest of CLAAC. We can't afford to let the opportunity go to waste."

"Yeah."

Bolan watched Bao, a hundred feet away at the entrance to gate 2, scan the arrivals monitor again. The sign had changed, indicating Malay 105 was in. He looked at Bolan across the vast space. Thomas Comas, the U.S. "expert," was arriving.

"Take position," Bolan said.

Jiahua walked through the terminal, directly behind Bao, the two of them not sparing each other a glance. She stood by a bench not far from the front main entrance, ignoring several cabbies and an interested young Malaysian man. Bolan caught her eye briefly over the distance. They were ready for whatever might happen.

Within ten minutes passengers of Malay 105 started filtering out of gate 2. Bolan assessed each carefully: a few tourists, some Malaysians and Taiwanese nationals, a couple of U.S. businessmen. Then he spotted a worried, balding man in his late forties with a bulging canvas garment bag and a cheap briefcase. Nothing obvious told Bolan he was their man; he nevertheless guessed that this was Comas, if Comas really was an American reactor expert. Sure enough, he spotted Bao, who was holding a sign made from a large white envelope. They greeted each other stiffly. Comas didn't seem to know Bao. The Chinese agent politely took the garment bag and they headed for the exit.

Bolan scratched his temple briefly, a signal that sent Jiahua out the front entrance ahead of Bao and Comas. The Executioner fell in step behind them, maintaining a twenty-five-foot cushion. Comas wasn't aware of his tail. In fact, he gave the appearance of being almost a bumbler. He was fumbling with his briefcase, looking around the airport as if he'd never seen a foreign country, staring at the Malaysians with a suspicious, almost frightened demeanor. He seemed nervous and uncomfortable.

It might be an act, Bolan knew. Comas might be a consummate professional.

They exited the airport and crossed to the parking lot where Bao's boxy Daihatsu was parked. Jiahua was thirty seconds ahead of them and was starting the Suburban. Bolan timed his pace carefully, arriving at the Suburban as Bao and Comas were pulling from their spot and heading toward the exit. But he was convinced by then that Comas was oblivious to anything occurring around him.

Bolan jumped in the driver's seat of the Suburban just as Jiahua slid over to the passenger side and tuned up the listening device. A bug had been planted in Bao's vehicle, part of the stash of equipment the two CIA agents had kept on hand.

Nervous American chatter emerged from the speaker. Bolan knew who it was immediately.

"Never been to Malaysia. Heard it's really starting to open up to American business, though. Heard they're really getting their act together here. But you still can't drink the water."

"Mr. Comas, I was informed by Mr. Lung that you would be providing the address of our destination."

"What's that? Oh, yes. Chiang said I was supposed to tell you where to go. Hope it isn't far from here. Doesn't this box have any air-conditioning?"

"No. Do you have the address?"

"Yeah." There was the metallic click. Bolan pictured the briefcase latches opening. The Daihatsu, a light blue, well-beaten rental car, was pulling onto a narrow highway, merging with frantic Sungai Petani traffic. He followed at a hundred yards, confident with Comas's ignorance. He heard more activity in the car over the speaker, then the rustling of paper.

"We're supposed to go to another airport. I can't say the name of the town or of the street it's on, but I wrote it down. Here."

A moment later Bao was obviously reading off the note Comas was showing him. "The town is Kuala Kampung. The street name is Reganua. It should be easy enough to find. Kuala Kampung is small. It can't have more than one airport. It cannot be a very large airport at that."

"Good. The quicker the better," Comas said with some relief. "How far've we got to go do you figure?"

"Kuala Kampung is about 250 miles from here. I would imagine we will get there within five hours."

The tiny speaker buzzed with the burst of expletives from Comas. "Five hours?" the American shouted. "In this damned little box without air-conditioning? You've got to be kidding."

Jiahua was grinning. "I have a feeling Mr. Comas isn't going to particularly enjoy his first visit to Malaysia."

Comas proceeded to rant for a good five minutes. "Why the hell didn't Lung just have me fly into this damned Kuala Kampung airport in the first place?"

"I don't think he realized he would be there. We have just moved out of Sungai Petani in the last day, and it was an unplanned move. Do you know nothing of this?"

"No, I don't know anything about it. I was told I'd be meeting up with him in Sungai Petani and I would be moving with them only in the next week or so after the plans were drawn up."

"When did you get his address?" Bao asked.

"Hank Chiang called me just yesterday. How come you didn't know anything about it?"

"Our security is tight even internally, Mr. Comas. For obvious reasons."

Bolan was increasingly satisfied with Wai Bao's performance. He was drawing whatever information he could out of Thomas Comas, which obviously was precious little. He was, for all practical purposes, giving the Executioner everything he could. But the soldier also knew he couldn't yet trust the Chinese agent. Not fully. But trust was something he seldom gave anyone in substantial degrees.

They hit the highway, which they would follow northeast along the Malaysia-Thailand border. The highway would reach the South China Sea and then turn southeast, more or less following the coast, around the city of Kota Bharu and on to Kuala Kampung. The late-afternoon sun was hot, but would be down before too long. They had a long drive ahead of them.

BOLAN STAYED MILES behind the little Daihatsu. Even certain as he was that Comas was oblivious to his tail, he didn't want to chance being spotted by him—or by any watch that might have been sent by Lung to keep an eye on Wai Bao.

More than once they listened as Bao tried to extract information out of Comas. He asked the American where he came from, what he did for a living. Comas's replies were noncommittal. Bao asked him if he was from L.A.

"You ask a lot of damned questions," Comas replied. Bolan hoped Bao knew when to quit.

"I apologize, Mr. Comas. It is just that I am very interested in how people live in America. I have never been there. CLAAC will help make China like America."

"Yeah, sure," Comas muttered.

"You don't believe CLAAC will succeed?"

"Don't know and don't care."

"But how come you have agreed to help us if you do not believe in the righteousness of CLAAC's ideals?"

"Cash, my friend. Cold and hard and right out of Hank Chiang's bank account. And I have some serious debts to pay off. Now, if you don't mind, I might as well use this time to try and get some sleep."

IT WAS 2:00 a.m. when Bolan heard Wai Bao speak again over the speaker. "Mr. Comas, we are entering Kuala Kampung. We'll be at the airport shortly."

The Daihatsu was approximately a mile and a half ahead of the Suburban. Sure enough, it was less than two minutes later when he saw the sign for Kuala Kampung. Jiahua had been sleeping, as well, but woke up at the sound of Bao's voice. They moved in closer on the Daihatsu, since it was easier to appear like regular traffic in the midst of the town even though the streets were all but deserted. The houses and neighborhoods on the outskirts of the town weren't wired for electricity and were utterly dark.

It wasn't long before the Daihatsu pulled up to the garage entrance of an airplane hangar at the edge of the Kuala Kampung municipal airport. The building was dark, but it matched the address Comas had supplied. Wai Bao stepped out of the car as Bolan drove past in the Suburban, turned the next corner and halted quickly. He exited the vehicle as quietly as possible and stepped to the corner of the building that blocked them from the view of the hangar.

The door was opened almost immediately when Bao knocked. There was no light inside, but in the quiet city the sound of their voices traveled well enough for the soldier to recognize spoken Mandarin. Bao got back in the Daihatsu, and the garage door opened just long enough to allow the car to pull into the darkness.

Jiahua had been listening on the tuner. "Anything?" Bolan asked, getting back in the vehicle.

"Nothing of note. They're just getting out."

A greeting was spoken in Chinese, then the sound of car doors closing. Bao had left his window open, so the conversation was still audible.

"They're explaining to Wai Bao—there's a car ready to leave right away with Comas," Jiahua translated. "Bao is to stay here in Kuala Kampung. He'll leave with the rest of them in the morning."

"I don't like the sound of that."

"Me, neither. What can we do, though?"

"Not a thing."

They heard Bao explain the situation to Comas, who complained vigorously. The last thing he wanted to do was sit in a car again for another several hours. But these were Kao Lung's orders, and the man relented. A moment later they heard the garage door open, and another car, with Comas in the back seat and a Chinese at the wheel, exited and drove off through town.

The voices coming through the receiver in Bao's car were retreating rapidly. A moment later they were gone.

"We should have bugged him," Jiahua said.

"Too risky. They might be searching him at this very moment if they question his loyalty even the slightest."

"So? What's the next move?"

Bolan glanced at the car clock. 2:11 a.m. "We wait."

THEY PULLED OUT of the alley and traveled down the street another hundred feet, where the road inclined and provided a good view of the hangar and the street. Kuala Kampung's airport didn't operate at night, so was silent. The street was mostly businesses and over the several hours that followed they saw only occasional rats and a dog.

The sound of a gunshot was so loud it nearly blew out the tuner speaker. Bolan heard it just as clearly through the open window. Jiahua was startled awake.

"What was that?"

"Get down." The street became glaringly illuminated as the garage door opened, and seconds later a microbus and a flatbed truck pulled out quickly, one after another. The bus appeared to contain only a driver and one passenger, the truck only a driver.

"Shouldn't we go after them?"

"No. I'm guessing Wai Bao isn't in those trucks. We can't leave him here. Anything he might have learned in the past couple of hours might be valuable."

"I think we ought to follow those trucks."

"I don't."

Bolan opened the door to the Suburban as the last taillight disappeared around a distant corner and dragged his backpack over one arm. "I'm going in."

"What'll I do?"

"Be prepared."

"For what?"

"Anything."

He slipped down the street, deep in the shadows, glancing back once to the Suburban. He couldn't see Jiahua's face but knew she was fuming. Maybe she thought he was a sexist pig. Maybe she was dwelling on any rumors she might have heard from the CIA heads who gave her this assignment. The CIA had its own peculiar opinion of Bolan.

Regardless of her opinion of him, he would not compromise himself or this mission.

He listened at the door to the hangar.

6

Men Qiu was startled by his name being blared over the loudspeaker, and his last shot went wild. But a wild shot from him was as precise as some of the best shots from the other agents in the firing range. He didn't bother to check his grouping—six shots dead center in the paper target figure's chest, six in the skull and the one aberrant shot in the throat.

He raced to his commander's office immediately. Upon entering, he was immediately berated. "What is the meaning of keeping me waiting, Men Qiu?"

He didn't recognize the man who spoke, but he bore the insignia of a Commander.

"I apologize, Commander. I was on the shooting range and came here as fast—"

"Why did you bring your gun into my presence? Are you deliberately trying to insult me?"

"No, Commander!" It was at that moment Men Qiu saw the curled, scarred right hand of the man and knew to whom he was speaking—Zhao Li, who had been one of the finest agents in the secret service. The loss of his right hand was the result of an attempt to fire an improperly assembled experimental Chinese rifle. He no longer had the muscle in that hand to work a simple trigger—or to do anything else. It now hung limp and useless. "I am sorry. No insult was intended."

Li wasn't satisfied and intended to continue his tirade, but at that instant Commander Xin entered the room.

"Good morning, Men Qiu. I see you have met Commander Zhao Li. Commander, this is Men Qiu, the finest sharpshooter in the employ of the Chinese secret service. And a good agent."

"He strikes me as being insolent and uncooperative," Li said flatly.

"Nonsense. That is your own bitterness talking, Commander."

Li fumed silently as Xin sat at his desk. "Do you not even wish to consider him for your team?"

"I will consider him."

"Qiu, Commander Li is leading a four-man team that will be leaving for Malaysia within the hour. The mission is vital to the lives of hundreds of thousands of Chinese citizens."

Qiu's interest was instantly aroused.

"I need someone with your training," Li began.

"A sharpshooter," Xin added.

Li glared at the other officer. "Yes. And your commander has recommended you. As you can hear, he thinks highly of your abilities. Do you have anything to say for yourself?"

Qiu wondered if he was being complimented or challenged. "I have tried my best sir, and would do my best on this mission if chosen."

Li raised his eyebrows. "No more to say than that?"

"What would you like to know, sir?"

"He's an insolent puppy, Xin, just like the rest of your agents."

"If you don't want him, then that is fine. But you have no reason to insult my men and myself. Good morning." Xin stood and opened the door.

"Just a moment . . ."

"I'm not going to haggle with you, Xin. This is one of the finest agents in the service. He isn't a sack of rice being sold in the market. He will also not grovel at your feet as penance for insult and disrespect perceived by you and no one else. If you wish to discuss my granting you the privilege of using this agent, then we shall do so. But that is the only agenda we shall discuss."

"All right. Let's discuss it."

Qiu knew he would be opening himself up for trouble by joining Commander Li's team. He had always been a tough man, with a reputation for flying off the handle without obvious cause and taking out his anger on his agents. Since his accident, which left him without his claim to fame—his own sharpshooting skills had been well-known for years— he had become more belligerent and nearly impossible to work for.

On the other hand, seldom would Men Qiu get an opportunity to work on a high-prestige case such as the one outlined to him. He would be traveling to Malaysia, tracking down one of the most dangerous antigovernment factions that had developed. When he heard about CLAAC's intentions, his blood ran cold.

"Agent Wai Bao has been unable to get word to us for some time. We didn't even realize the group had moved to Malaysia and, quite frankly, we were convinced Bao had changed loyalties," Commander Xin said. "Then he got word out via the CIA—apparently U.S. agents have successfully tracked down the group to Malaysia and are working with Bao to locate CLAAC's Malaysian base of operations. Once we find that, we believe, we'll find the hardware and the personnel the group plans on using to break into our reactors here in China."

"We're going in to find it," Li said. "Once there, we will wipe out CLAAC, its hardware and its support staff. Hopefully the U.S. agents, as well."

"Why would we take out the CIA, sir?" Qiu asked.

"We have *not* been authorized to take out the CIA agents involved in the case," Xin said deliberately, looking directly at Li as he spoke. "However, we do believe one of the U.S. agents is the man responsible for foiling a raid we attempted last week on Hang Chiang, the U.S. businessman financing CLAAC. Ninety percent of the personnel we sent on that mission were lost."

Qiu was stunned. He said nothing for a moment, then realized no one was speaking. "Why would the U.S. protect Chiang?"

"They wanted him alive so they could get CLAAC's whereabouts from him."

"Were we attempting the same thing?"

"Are you questioning our tactics?" Li demanded.

"No, sir. I am trying simply to understand the situation as it has come about to this point."

"You don't need to understand it. You will not be in charge of it. In fact, you will be at the bottom of the seniority ladder if you take this assignment. Will you take it?"

"Yes, sir. I am honored to be asked."

"Be ready to leave in thirty minutes." Li rose and left the office.

"Watch out for that dog," Commander Xin said quietly. "Watch out for yourself, Men Qiu. I'm only loaning you to Zhao Li and I want you back."

BOLAN PRESSED HIS EAR to the door to the hangar and detected only silence. Then he noticed a black substance seeping out from under it. In the absence of streetlights or visible moon, it nonetheless glimmered. It might have been oil or even water, but Bolan had seen enough spilled blood in his life to know it when he saw it. The trickle from inside the hangar had created a puddle fully a foot in diameter. He connected it to the gunshot heard minutes before.

The soldier circled the side of the building to an eight-foot chain-link fence that he scaled easily, flopping to the ground on airport property. He doubted the airport had any security measures other than the fence itself. But he was more careful as he approached the rear windows of the hangar. Chiang's money could have paid for the installation of a high-tech, sophisticated warning system. Peering through the dingy glass into darkness, he spotted the gleaming red pinpoint of a laser perimeter.

The hangar door for aircraft was too large to open easily, even if it was unlocked, and would make a racket if he tried it. The window was the best option as it was designed to slide down to open. Bolan dragged on it with all his weight until it lurched open with a grating sound of wood on wood.

He climbed onto the sill and waited, but he heard nothing. He jumped over the laser beam, shoes scraping on the concrete when he landed, and froze.

There was a second security system, one he wasn't supposed to find—the realization had come to him in the moment he was airborne over the tiny red beam. The obviousness of the beam had been a gnawing concern, almost subconsciously disturbing him since he'd noticed it. As still as rigid death in the dark hangar, he waited for some reaction. Motion detectors, sound sensors, video monitors—any type of electronic surveillance might have just been triggered.

Nothing happened. Bolan knew that simply because he couldn't see or hear it didn't mean he hadn't alerted an electronic watchdog of some type, which was even now barking furiously in the form of an alarm somewhere. His safest course of action would be to flee immediately. Instead, he proceeded into the interior of the hangar.

The entire structure was illuminated by a single exit sign over the front door, leaving Bolan able to make out little as he made his way across the empty bay to Wai Bao's Daihatsu. The man lay behind his vehicle.

He'd been shot just above the knee on the inside of the leg and had fallen with one hand reaching out, almost touching the front garage door of the hangar. That was only the most recent of his wounds. He had been stripped to his trousers, and his back was covered with bruises, cuts, scrapes and dried blood. Bao's cover had been blown somehow. Bolan realized at once that the agent had been shot deliberately so that he wouldn't die, or at least not appear dead. He stood over the agent a long moment before chancing the use of his penlight.

Bolan crouched to the ground, carefully lifted Bao's right arm from the concrete floor and peered underneath him. The man's chest, or what he could see of it, was also covered in cuts and slashes, and his face was nearly black with bruises. A small grenade was tied with wire to the front of his pants, the pin ring attached to another piece of wire knotted to a rusty nail driven into the concrete. Bolan had found the second security system he had suspected.

They knew more than that Bao was an infiltrator. They knew he had friends and that those friends were probably watching him, would probably come looking for him once they heard the gunshot.

Did that mean they knew about the bug? Or had they hoped the gunshot itself would be loud enough to be heard, assuming Bao's companions would be in close proximity? Bolan made a quick search of the Daihatsu and found the device still wired securely under the driver's seat. He extracted it.

"Cello, it's Belasko," he said into the device. "There's going to be an explosion in a minute. Don't worry. I'll be out of the way. But I think our friends in the vehicles will return very shortly after it goes off. I could use a distraction about five minutes after they get here."

He had no way of knowing if she had heard him. If the device was working—and if she had stayed in the Suburban—she would have. Stuffing the bug into his pocket, he attached a length of rope from his backpack to Bao's body, then looked for a decent hiding place. He decided on the rafters. Once the explosion occurred, the hanging rafter lights would be blown out, and he would remain more or less in darkness no matter what other lights they turned on. He threw the long end of the rope over the rafter and climbed up both ends at once, scrambling onto the rust-flaked steel rafter. He walked with the rope as far away as he could, then pulled on it, hard enough to flop over Bao's body.

The delay on the grenade, as he had assumed, was short. One second later it exploded, filling the interior of the hangar with light and sound, and making a massive impact against the Daihatsu, which crumpled. The hangar door, which distended into the street, was torn open in places.

Making his way forward, Bolan crouched over the spot where Bao's corpse had been. Minutes later headlights shone through the rips in the garage door, which was yanked open. The microbus and the flatbed truck were back. Three Chinese stood in the street with drawn handguns.

Bolan waited for them to bring their vehicle back into the garage. The Chinese weren't cooperating. They stood investigating the carnage, attempting, he assumed, to determine how many bodies were actually left in the ruin. A gunshot distracted them. Jiahua, eager to get into the action, hadn't waited five minutes. More like two. There wasn't much he could do about it now. The Chinese scrambled behind their vehicles as bullets peppered the open street.

Firing her Colt All American, she shattered one of the rear windows in the microbus and poked holes in its side panel, then bounced a 9 mm parabellum round off the roof of the flatbed truck cab, making a lot of noise but doing little serious damage. After nine shots her firing ceased. The Chinese jumped out from behind their cover and started in her direction, blasting at her. Bolan, wondering if his CIA companion had bitten off more than she could chew, dropped his safety rope to the ground and scrambled down. There was no time to worry about Jiahua. He raced to the street, diving through the open door without checking to see if any of the Chinese, for whatever reason, were looking back. The Executioner somersaulted and was back on his feet, now protected by the rear end of the flatbed. He scrambled to the cab, finding the driver's door wide open, and jammed the bugging device underneath the seat, attaching its securing clips to the springs. It would be easy enough to find if they started looking for it. He would have to hope they didn't.

A glance out the window showed the Suburban far up the road and roaring away in the other direction, the Chinese firing after it. It was going to be just seconds before they gave up and headed back to the vehicles, and surely they knew the local police were on their way by this time.

Bolan paused just long enough to grab at the tarpaulin that was protecting the pile of cargo on the flatbed, revealing a substantial stack of rectangular boxes. He grabbed one and yanked it open. Inside were brick-sized squares of slate gray, maleable dough. Bolan knew immediately what it was—C-4 plastique.

He just wasn't sure he'd ever seen so much of it in one spot. The brick of plastic explosive in his hand could destroy a house. The truckload could level a small town, or crack the adamantine seal on a nuclear reactor.

Bolan had discovered the primary ingredient in CLAAC's recipe for Chinese nuclear genocide.

There was a screech, and the Suburban halted at an angle in the street. Jiahua, half-protected by the vehicle, stood over the top of it, bringing her Heckler & Koch MP-5 A-5 submachine gun into play. She aimed it carefully above the three Chinese and shot off a 3-round burst, showering them with pulverized concrete from a nearby building. The enemy adopted firing stances, and another hail of bullets impacted the Suburban. Bolan heard the faraway tinkle of glass as he ducked into a narrow alley on the other side of the street. He made his way to the next parallel street, jogging several blocks until he could hear the blasts from Jiahua's weapon parallel to him, then cut through another alley to rejoin the fray.

By that time the Chinese had retreated to the cover of their own vehicles again.

"Let's get out of here," Bolan said from the far side of the street.

Jiahua turned on him in surprise. "Where the hell did you come from?"

"We can't stand around here firing at one another all night. The cops are going to be showing up here pretty soon. I don't want to have to deal with the local law enforcement."

She hopped back in the Suburban and pulled farther up the street, until the Chinese were hidden from view. Bolan climbed in while she was in the midst of the three-point turn, and they raced back in the direction of the Chinese. The CLAAC hardmen had already returned to their own vehicles and were racing away in the other direction.

"What's the deal, Belasko?"

"Bao's dead. They tortured him, then they shot him."

"Dammit," she said quietly.

"They booby-trapped his body. They wanted his comrades to sneak in and find him still alive, move his body to try to help him and set off a grenade. They thought they could keep him alive and unconscious by shooting him in the leg. Only they struck his artery. He bled to death in minutes. I set off the explosion after I recovered your bug and was able to get it tucked into the truck while you had them distracted."

"You set off the explosion deliberately?"

The soldier didn't answer.

"What happened to Bao?"

"You've never seen what happens when a man dives on a hand grenade?"

Even in the dim light of Kuala Kampung, she blanched noticeably. "That's not too respectful, Belasko."

"Bao didn't mind. And it accomplished what it was supposed to accomplish."

"You are one cold bastard."

Bolan ignored the remark and turned up the volume on the tuner. There had been nothing but background static coming from it, but now he heard voices speaking Chinese.

"They're arguing over how many of us there were back there," Jiahua said. "They think they killed one of us. Yeah, they think one of us died in the explosion." There was a pause, followed by another excited burst of conversation.

"They saw only me in the Suburban. They think I'm the only one left."

"Good."

She smiled humorously. "Since I'm a woman, they don't seem to think I'm too much of a threat. One of them just called me the Chinese equivalent of a bimbo."

"Even better. Maybe they won't even expect you to pursue them. But what we need is their destination. I doubt they'll head back to the hangar, and anyway it obviously was not CLAAC's primary base of operations."

"They haven't said anything about it—wait." She pulled the Suburban to the side of the road as more conversation came from the tuner. Head cocked to one side, she grinned.

"Someplace called Ompang," she said, yanking the steering wheel, sharply sending the truck into a U-turn that sent them back into the city. "They're going to Ompang."

Bolan grabbed the detailed map of Malaysia in the glove compartment of the Suburban. It took him a full minute to locate a tiny dot called Ompang—a village wedged in the rain forests of peninsular Malaysia's southeastern end. He pointed it out to his companion.

"Kuala Kampung was just a staging area on the route between Sungai Petani and Ompang," she said.

Bolan agreed. "Ompang has to be a good five-hour drive from here. That gives us plenty of time to destroy their cargo."

"Which is?"

"Plastique. Hundred of pounds of it. Very dangerous in those quantities. Unbelievably dangerous in the hands of CLAAC, if they ever do manage to get it inside a reactor somehow. The percussive force could shatter reactor containment and allow the radiation inside to pour out. The only way to stop it would be to construct a dome of concrete over it, like they did in Chernobyl. And nobody would be able to get close enough for that until days or weeks after the disaster."

"Aren't reactors' safety systems designed to handle just such an emergency?"

"Reactor safety systems are designed to handle cracks or leaks. We're talking about a pulverized reactor casing—containment that has been entirely compromised," he said. "Imagine what's left when you drop a fishbowl."

7

Dawn over northern peninsular Malaysia was a brilliant mix of orange and red, and as soon as the day was bright enough to kill the headlights and make the Suburban less obvious, Bolan pulled to within a quarter mile of the microbus. The flatbed with its deadly cargo wasn't much farther ahead.

"Are we going to tail them all the way to Ompang?" Jiahua asked.

"No. We have to blow that cargo. I have a feeling they're going to have air transportation waiting in Ompang to get their supplies inside China. That means right now is our last good opportunity to take it out."

"That also means we won't have any way of finding CLAAC's base. And what if they have more explosives there? What if this does turn out to be our last chance to track down Lung and Chiang?"

"I'm hoping we'll be able to find their base some other way."

"Ompang may be a tiny Malaysian backwater, Belasko, but the area of jungle around is massive and the compound could be hidden anywhere. I don't know how we're going to find it if you blow up the guys who might lead us there. Unlike in Alor Setar, we don't have any EastStar street addresses to go looking for. We're going to look pretty damned stupid hanging out at Ompang Chinese restaurants until we run across familiar faces."

"Then we look stupid. Those explosives are not going to reach their destination, Jiahua."

She said nothing for a long moment. The sun was rising above the landscape fully and flashing directly in their faces.

"You don't even need to get the okay from your boss, do you? You just get to go in and start blowing things up. Who the hell do you work for, anyway, Belasko?"

Bolan said nothing.

THEIR CHANCE CAME within minutes. As they crossed over a hilltop on the highway and started down a long slope, they spotted the microbus and flatbed truck parked beside a ramshackle gasoline station and grocery store. One of the Chinese was sitting on the bumper of the microbus eating a candy bar while two others guzzled bottles of soda. Jiahua kept driving, and Bolan sank out of sight. By the time they spotted the Chinese, it was too late for any other course of action. A sudden stop on their part would have instantly attracted the enemy's attention. In the daylight the vehicle's battle scars were clear, and it would have taken only a passing look for the Chinese terrorist to realize the Suburban driving past them on the highway was *the* Suburban. Bolan looked back as soon as they had driven by and tried to discern any sudden urgency in the behavior of the terrorist. Nothing.

"Pull off as soon as we're out of sight," he said. "What have you got in the way of explosives?"

"I've got a flare gun. Why not just blast the truck long-distance?"

"That won't do it. C-4 is highly powerful stuff, but it needs to be detonated. We need a small explosion—not just a fire—to be absolutely sure we start a major explosion. And then we have to be able to get away fast."

She pulled off the road, raising a cloud of dust. A large rise in the land was now between them and the gas station at the top of the hill.

"The grenades I've got get pretty damned hot."

She was referring to her stock of AN-M14 hand grenades. Pretty damn hot, indeed, Bolan thought. They burned on the order of 2,200° Celsius for a full half minute.

"Exactly what I was thinking." He got out and began to sort through the contents of the canvas duffels in the rear of the vehicle.

"How you're going to set the thing off is another matter," Jiahua continued, joining him. "Its delay is five seconds. That's the problem. If this plastique is as powerful as you claim, you won't have time to get to a safe distance."

Bolan nodded. He had been thinking along those lines himself. "I'll have to get behind one of those hills during the delay. Unless you've got some way of blowing this from a distance."

"No, I don't. And I seriously doubt you'll be able to get yourself behind any mountain during a five-second delay."

The soldier transferred the grenade to his backpack and hoisted it over one shoulder. "Then you won't have anybody around anymore telling you how to run things."

He jogged in the direction of the gas station, keeping the hill between himself and it, hoping the geography would cooperate until he was well behind the building. It didn't. The rise fell away and left him standing in a field, dangerously exposed, no potential shelter to be found. His best hope lay in the unlikelihood any of the Chinese would be looking for him, especially coming from behind the gas station.

His luck was good as he continued on to the gas station, an easy half mile, approaching it from the rear. He caught a glimpse of the two vehicles in the lot, and hoped they weren't going to be leaving in the next two or three minutes.

He yanked open the rear door of the tiny store with the Beretta 93-R drawn, and moved into a back utility room, finding it empty. There was no door between it and the rest of the building. Bolan stepped into the store and found a Chinese hardman pulling another soda from an ancient refrigerator. With a glance at the Executioner he yelped something in Mandarin, dropped the bottle of cola and threw himself backward behind a large, sagging wooden grocery shelf. Bolan fired quickly at the only part of the man still exposed, his right foot. The foot gushed blood and the man screamed. A volley of bullets tore into the ceiling from what sounded like an automatic handgun.

Bolan sank to the floor in a crouch, crawled around the cabinet in the other direction while more bullets from the gunner crashed through the top of the shelf where he had been standing, flinging bottles of headache tablets to the floor. The soldier peered around the shelf. He and the Chinese terrorist achieved eye contact in the same instant. The enemy brought down his handgun without removing his finger from the trigger, and it was cutting a path of .308-caliber destruction through the shelf when Bolan aimed the Beretta and fired once into the man's skull, coring his brain.

The others would have been alerted by the gunfire, and Bolan wanted more stopping power to deal with them. It took just seconds for him to tuck away the handgun and arm himself with the larger Desert Eagle, and in those seconds he had risen to his feet. A blast from outside cut a neat hole in a window. One of the Chinese was bracing his firing arm on his wrist as he paced steadily in the direction of the shack. He fired again after glimpsing Bolan, the round searing the air above the soldier's head, but he had descended again into a crouch. The big American assessed the man's position and fired through the wall of the shack. The .44 Magnum round punched through the layer of flimsy wooden wall, and Bolan clearly heard a grunt. He was on his feet instantly and vaulted through the front door of the shack. The gunner was down but not out. His gut was a mess of blood, but the wooden wall had slowed the Magnum round enough so that the terrorist hadn't been instantly killed. His eyes were contemptuous but clouded by pain. He attempted to use the gun, leveling it as before on his other wrist. Bolan blasted him again, and he was eviscerated.

An elderly Malaysian man was crouched against the building in the fetal position, and he looked at Bolan utterly terrified. The soldier waved the Desert Eagle at the building. "Get inside."

The man didn't know the English words but nevertheless comprehended and did as instructed, hobbling into the building. Bolan had forgotten him already as he searched for the third Chinese. At that moment the flatbed truck, no driver in evidence, started to roll.

Bolan fired into the cab of the vehicle, the Desert Eagle creating four huge holes in the metal without affecting its increasing pace. Then it bounced onto the road. The driver was crouched on the seat, peeking above the dash. He adjusted his course for the sloping, slightly curving highway and stomped on the gas. The soldier was already running, and he grabbed at the rear of the vehicle just before it shifted gears and surged ahead. He was yanked off his feet and felt the heat of instant friction as his shoes scraped viciously against the asphalt.

He was gripping a shaft of rusty metal on the rear of the truck and made a quick grab for a flapping end of the canvas tarpaulin. Once he had it, he dragged himself up, hand over hand, then flung a leg onto the flatbed. He found himself momentarily safe and, crouching low, proceeded to the front of the bed.

The driver sat up fully in his seat, assuming his attacker was left behind. He corrected the swerving path of the truck, and at that moment drove past the parked Suburban. He had to have recognized the vehicle, or the young woman at the wheel, and that roused his suspicions, because he suddenly half stood in his seat and looked through the rear window of the cab. It was the only way he could have spotted Bolan. The driver grabbed a gun from the seat next to him and twisted awkwardly to fire through the window. Glass rained on Bolan, who aimed the Desert Eagle at a tough angle and returned fire. The blast missed the driver, and the man's second volley of shots blasted out the rear window. Neither of them could reach an angle that would allow a clear shot without exposing themselves.

Bolan jumped to the driver's side of the bed and reached around to the open window of the cab for a handhold, then swung himself bodily along the driver's-side door, standing on the rickety running board. The hardman gaped in surprise, but with instant reflexes snapped his elbow at the gripping hand. The reaction was nearly perfect and had the effect of almost lifting the soldier's fingers away from the window. But without enough leverage, the blow was ineffective and Bolan's grip held. He fired the Desert Eagle directly into the driver's neck, tearing away a substantial portion of his spine.

The truck swerved off the road in the direction of a ravine. Bolan transferred his grip from the window to the steering wheel in a snatching movement and yanked the truck back onto the asphalt. He holstered the Desert Eagle and surveyed the landscape ahead.

The ravine paralleled the highway about ten yards off to the right, and as they neared the bottom of the hill he saw it grew deeper. Not much cover, he estimated, but it was about all he had available. He withdrew the AN-M14 grenade while swerving the truck to reduce its speed. Gravity and the high gear the late driver had put the vehicle in conspired against him. The end of the hill was getting closer, and the Executioner's time was running short. He let go of the steering wheel and swung himself back onto the bed. The truck was already drifting to the right. He wondered if it would stay on the road long enough to travel the minimal distance needed to keep the explosive force from ripping him to shreds.

Wedging the grenade under one of the canvas's rope restraints he yanked the pin and stepped to the edge of the bed. The wheels were rolling on the shoulder of the road, raising a cloud of dust, and he couldn't see the lay of the land. It was a fast-moving, indistinguishable blur. Bolan stepped into it and experienced a blasting impact that flung him into an uncontrollable roll, rattling the bones in his body like sticks in a can. Then with a massive smashing sensation he stopped. It took another fraction of a second for his orientation to return and to realize he had been halted by a low mass of rock. He sprang with energy he didn't have to the other side of the boulder. As he hit the ground, an earthquake began and rumbled all around him, and the morning oranges and reds were drowned out by a piercing, burning white light that filled the vast Malaysian valley.

Where the truck had been was a patch of smoking, charred earth, surrounded at a distance by twisted shards and hunks of smoldering metal. The spot had the utterly destroyed look of ground zero.

With a squeak of brakes, the Suburban came gradually to a halt fifty feet away. Jiahua stepped out of the vehicle slowly but stayed behind the protective shelter of the door, gazing at the ruin.

Bolan was shaking off the worst of the jarring experience with full knowledge he was going to feel sore for quite some time.

"You all right, Belasko? I can't believe you're even walking."

"Yeah. I'll live. Let's get out of here."

KAO LUNG LIFTED the television and the aluminum cart it was sitting on and threw them as far as he could. The cathode-ray tube made a hollow, imploding sound when it hit the nearby wall, then the entire mass descended to the floor with a crashing and crunching of metal and glass. Hank Chiang entered the room and regarded the mess with a grimace.

Lung looked at him for a long minute. Neither man said a word. Chiang wouldn't broach the subject of Lung's anger, and Lung was busy trying to rein it in. He still needed Chiang—more correctly, his money and resources—and if he gave way to his temper, he would jump across the room and press his thumbs in Chiang's esophagus until he was a limp corpse.

It wasn't until the American, Thomas Comas, arrived that anything was said.

"Damn. What's going on?" he said.

"We've lost a shipment of plastique," Lung stated.

"Did the drivers call in?" Chiang asked.

"They did not call in. They have not called in since 6:00 a.m. And they were scheduled to report to me twice, at 8:00 and at 10:00 a.m."

"So how do you know—?"

"Malay television news reports an explosion on the coastal highway, two hundred miles northwest of here. On our drivers' route. A massive explosion, they say, far too intense to have been caused by a truck rupturing a tank of fuel. Plus the mystery of two Chinese at a nearby gas station shot dead. It makes for a pretty clear picture.''

Chiang folded his hands together, then pulled them apart. "I think my friend from the United States is still on our tail.''

"I thought your booby trap got him last night in Kuala Kampung,'' Comas said.

"I did, too!'' Chiang said. "What do you make of it?''

Lung shook his head very slightly. "I think you should have killed him when you had the chance.''

"How was I supposed to know what he was capable of, Kao?''

"You witnessed firsthand what he was capable of. You should have known better than to let him get away.''

"I tried to run him over with the truck! He was too damned slippery!''

"He's so 'slippery' he's infiltrated our compounds, seriously depleted our ranks here in Malaysia and now destroyed one-third of our supply of plastique. Your friend from the United States has done serious damage to this organization and its agenda.''

"We still have one load of plastique on-site,'' Chiang reminded him. "That's enough to shatter a reactor casing.''

"One reactor casing.''

"And you have our shipment coming in tonight,'' Comas added.

"That makes two. My plan specifically called for three simultaneous strikes. You've estimated yourself, Mr. Comas, that each of our teams will only have about a thirty-three percent chance of success. With three teams leading three attacks, then I am assured of at least one success. With two teams my chances of success are seriously compromised. I do not wish to be compromised.'' A large blue vein distended across Kao Lung's left temple, and his forehead had developed a sheen. His hands clenched again and again.

''Perhaps we could get one more shipment from Comas's people,'' Chiang suggested. ''I could get the money somehow. My personal accounts perhaps...''

''Mr. Comas, how long would it take for your people in the U.S. to send another two-hundred-pound shipment of plastique?''

Comas shrugged slightly. ''We don't have any more on hand. We'd have to procure it. Could take weeks to find a source for that much. We've more or less exhausted the sources we had.''

''Weeks. I don't have weeks,'' Lung said directly to Chiang. ''I have waited long enough, far too long, as it is. My plan called for our assaults to begin in three days. And I will not alter that schedule at this stage. We go with two teams.''

''But Kao—'' Chiang began.

''We go with two teams in three days. We will integrate the third team into the other two. We will reevaluate our plan and make changes for increased efficiency. We will improve our odds until we have reached at least a fifty percent chance for success with each team. I will not tolerate anything less than perfection. I will have my revenge on the government of the People's Republic!''

Chiang was nodding rapidly. ''Yes. Yes, Kao.''

Comas was sweating profusely. But it might just have been the oppressive heat of the Malaysian afternoon.

BOLAN REPORTED the situation succinctly, but in vague terms, over the line to Brognola's office at Stony Man Farm. The big Fed had already received reports of the explosion in central Malaysia that could only have been caused by a substantial portion of high explosives. "Knew you were mixed up in that mess somehow, Striker." He took Bolan's report, issued in code, and promised to have some data within the hour.

The Executioner and Jiahua continued their drive southwest, in the direction of Ompang, but when they stopped to call Brognola again his information caused them to change their destination.

"Thomas Comas—this guy's really in a downward spiral," the Justice man said. "Nuclear scientist. Two years ago he was the assistant director of one of the largest nuclear power-generating reactors in North America. Then his gambling hobby escalated into an addiction. Next thing you know, his wife divorced him and his banks were hounding him because he had two delinquent mortgages. He started borrowing from the Mob to feed his blackjack habit. Small-time stuff at first, graduating to triple-digit sums, which of course he can't pay. The Mafia gave him a choice—he either works for them until his bill is paid or they kill him and his family."

Bolan digested the story. It was tough to feel sorry for Comas. He was more or less responsible for throwing his own life into the toilet. But Brognola's comment about the Mafia threatening his family pushed buttons deep in the Executioner's gut.

"So he's on the Mafia's payroll," he said. "And they're selling his services to CLAAC."

"Yeah. Comas is now based out of Dallas, where he's linked to the Helms Family. They're becoming big-time and are very ambitious. Drugs, franchised prostitution and arms. They've been linked to the disappearance of some very dangerous high explosives. They're one-stop shopping for our Chinese friends. And get this—a Helms Family yacht left Honolulu ten days ago, bound for Malaysia and a port town called Hujan Kalantan. Supposedly it is a pleasure trip for one of the sons, a high-ranking Family member named Anthony Helms. I have a feeling we may have another shipment of your C-4 plastic explosive coming in."

"Sounds like it."

"I've had the yacht tracked by our Navy friends. They're traveling at 7.5 knots and could get into Hujan Kalantan by 4:00 a.m. tomorrow morning. No earlier than that. Perfect opportunity for a quick transfer of goods from the Helms yacht to waiting transport in Malaysia. They'd only be a few hours' drive to CLAAC's Ompang base. They'd be there in time for breakfast."

"That's our next target, then," Bolan said. "We can't let that shipment get to CLAAC. I'm going after it."

"And then?"

"I'll head to Ompang, locate the base and get rid of any plastique they may have already got on hand. I'll see what else I can do to slow them down."

"By the way, CIA is screaming about the death of their agent Chen Tian. They hold me—and you—personally responsible."

"Tell them I'll try to take better care of their second one." He hung up.

MEN QIU WALKED cautiously down the wharf, avoiding the coils of ropes and nets and the occasional piles of discarded fish parts. He had been marked instantly as a stranger by the fishermen of Hujan Kalantan, and no one spoke to him. He wasn't here for conversation anyway. He walked with deliberate slowness, observing the activity of the various crews. None appeared to be involved in abnormal activity.

Qiu left the wharf and crossed the street to a small market. He purchased a lukewarm bottle of cola, and ducked behind the ramshackle, salt-air-warped wooden building to drink it. He was hidden from sight except to anyone who walked through the alley. The agent watched the wall across the way grow dimmer as the sun drew nearer to the sea, turning after several minutes to check on the activity on the wharf. Nothing had changed. He glanced down the street in the other direction, to a small hotel. And that was when he spotted the American.

The man was leaving the hotel, walking across the small parking lot to a gray Suburban, and his companion was a beautiful, small Chinese woman who carried herself with a cockiness Qiu assumed marked her as being American, too. He corrected himself, watching her as she got into the vehicle. Some Chinese women native to Hong Kong and to Malaysia had the same self-assuredness, which he hadn't seen often in the women of mainland China. Whoever she was, she was undeniably quite attractive.

The two of them got into the Suburban and pulled onto the street, pointed away from Men Qiu's hiding spot. When they started up the street, he ran after them for a hundred yards before losing them. He swore, then reminded himself that he hadn't lost them for good. They appeared to be staying at that hotel. He could remain at his post and simply wait for them to return.

He sipped the soda so slowly it had gone flat before he finished it. By then the sun was halfway hidden by the South China Sea, and the night was getting darker. Activity had waned and nearly died on the wharf, the last of the fishermen storing their nets and checking the security of their fishing vessels before marching off through the streets to their homes in the village. A small group of them stopped by the grocery store and spotted Qiu leaning against its back wall. They muttered to him in Malaysian and walked by him deliberately close. The agent didn't take the bait, didn't meet their eyes or answer their words.

The locals might have been satisfied with a simple taunt and let it be. Qiu hoped such would be the case. But one of the older fishermen, with a face creased and brown like old, weathered leather, had been imbibing from his flask of liquor since his vessel reached the wharf. Clearly, he was itching for a fight and saw this as an opportunity to pick one before going home to his wife.

The fisherman told the stranger what he thought of him.

Qiu shrugged and told the old man he didn't understand.

"You are Chinese?" a younger man said in imperfect Mandarin. "My friend just told you you are a filthy pig."

Qiu nodded. "I expected no less."

"What are you going to do about it?"

"Nothing. What would you expect me to do about it?" He looked away, down the street, for any sign of the Suburban returning.

"You are not a pig, you are a woman!"

The Suburban had appeared. Qiu didn't answer the Malaysian but watched the vehicle pull into the hotel lot.

"You look at me when I'm talking to you, woman."

Qiu felt hands reaching in his direction. The man was going to do no more than touch him or shove him, a provocation for much more. Qiu snatched the young Malaysian's hand by the wrist and flopped it against the side of the building. It whipped into the wood, and at least one of the knuckles cracked.

The man screamed in Malaysian, and one of his friends stepped toward the agent. But Qiu had drawn his pistol. He found himself suddenly with a very wide berth, the Malaysians in a half circle around him, falling farther away.

"I would like to go back to leaning against this wall peacefully and undisturbed. Do you have a problem with that, my friend?"

The man with the cracked knuckles shook his head, and the group moved away into the night.

Qiu barely noticed them leaving, as he watched the American and his Chinese companion enter the small hotel together. Moments later he watched the lights go on in two of the rooms of the hotel. The agent felt a twinge of amusement when he realized the man and the attractive Chinese woman weren't in a room together.

He looked back to the wharf. It was all but deserted. An old man shuffled down the wooden dock, bent low, probably talking to himself. Qiu had observed him earlier and believed he dwelt in a tiny shack at the far end of the wharf.

There was another man, who appeared out of place. He sat at the prow of one of the fishing boats, doing nothing. Waiting. Qiu considered the man carefully, probing his memory of his earlier walk down the wharf. What activity had he noticed at this particular vessel? Any? He believed he remembered seeing the men untangling and repairing nets.

But they hadn't been unloading fish. He had assumed they were early arrivals, that they had unloaded before he had come to the dock. It was possible he was mistaken. Perhaps they hadn't gone fishing that day. Perhaps they had picked up other cargo or were planning to pick up other cargo later.

Qiu determined to keep an eye on the situation. But first he would check out his new lead. He crossed the street and headed in the direction of the tiny hotel.

By the time he reached the parking lot, the light in one of the rooms had gone out. He headed for the other room and stood outside, crouching in the weeds under the window.

The curtains were heavy and drawn. He glimpsed a smooth bare leg around the edge of the curtain and knew he wasn't at the American's room.

He stood in the weeds for ten minutes and in that time didn't hear a single word and saw nothing but shadows of movement from the room. Nothing of use.

Qiu walked down the street and crossed again, in the near-darkness of early night, to his vantage point at the small store. The business was closed, and there were no lights within. The wharf, across the dirt road, was also unlit. But the sea gave a kind of glimmering magnification to what starlight and moonlight there was, and Qiu found he could make out the movement on the wharf well enough.

He moved across the road cautiously, keeping to the shadows, and descended to damp, grassy ground at a rickety panel truck emblazoned with a fish-company name. He advanced on his stomach through the grass, snaking underneath the truck, ignoring the fishy muck he encountered. In a minute he had worked his way completely under the vehicle to the rear end, where he had an unobstructed view of the wharf and its nocturnal activity.

Observing the scene for a full five minutes convinced him he had found what he'd come to find. He wormed his way backward, crawling out from under the truck, and crept through the shadows away from the wharf. Zhao Li would by now be waiting for him to report. He would have good news for the commander.

Qiu didn't know that the activity on the wharf halted as soon as he left. A man on the roof of the very truck he had been crawling under watched him disappear from sight and waved to the men on the fishing vessel shortly. They prepared for the next phase of their operation.

8

Zhao Li listened to the extensive report, first about the arrival of the American then about the activity on the wharf, and there was a growing distress on his face.

"Are you sure this was the shipment of explosives being unloaded?" he asked while Qiu was in midsentence.

"No, Commander."

"Why not?"

"There were no markings on the cargo. All I know is that they did fit the description of the likely appearance of the plastique—small packages of boxed material. They appeared quite heavy, and the pickup truck they were loaded into was riding low when I left, and it was just half-loaded."

"A good agent would have made sure of what he saw before he reported it."

"I had no way of doing so, Com—"

"Fah!" Li silenced him with a wave of his clawed hand. "You don't make my decision easy by giving me incomplete information and a child's excuses!"

Qiu was silent for a moment, then said levelly, "Perhaps if you were to go yourself and make the determination . . ."

"Quiet! You're an insubordinate fool! I should have known better than to recruit one of Xin's pampered, incompetent morons!"

Qiu bowed his head and said nothing. Li's tirade went no further, for at that moment Yuan Mei and Wu Jian, the other two agents on the team, arrived at the Mercedes from their own rounds. They reported only that they had seen nothing.

"Men Qiu has found what may or may not be an important lead. He neglected to procure enough information to know for sure. Qiu, repeat your report."

The agent related again what he had seen, adding that he wasn't certain the cargo was indeed the plastique.

The other agents were experienced with Li's modus operandi and read the truth easily through what Qiu had said. No agent could have been able to determine for certain what was in the cargo. Qiu had simply reported as best he could what he had seen. But that information left Li with a tough choice: devote the extremely limited resources of the team to following up on the report or continue canvassing the village.

Li drove in the direction of the wharf, killing the lights on the Mercedes and halting a good distance away. There was no activity visible from the street. The commander ordered Qiu to check on the situation quickly. The young agent was glad to get out of the uncomfortable atmosphere of the Mercedes, but he returned as soon as he saw what was going on at the wharf.

"The fishermen are leaving their ship, and the pickup truck looks like it is fully loaded and ready to depart," he said. "Here they come."

Now they could see the fishermen who had been unloading the vessel emerging from the dock and walking into the village, laborers on their way home from work later than usual. Then the headlights of the pickup followed them out. There was a mound of cargo in the bed, covered and roped in. It turned in the opposite direction and started up the street.

A decision now had to be made, but Li didn't seem to be making it. He was breathing deeply, playing with his crippled hand as if it were a pet that gave him comfort. "You've put me in a bad situation, Qiu!" he blurted suddenly.

Qui didn't respond.

"All right, we go after the pickup. But you will stay here!" His clawed hand pointed viciously to the street. "You keep an eye on that American. Shoot him dead if you get the chance. You might as well kill his female, as well."

"Commander, our orders are—"

"Quiet! I'll not be reminded of orders from the likes of you! Get out of this car! Check your radio every fifteen minutes for my contact."

"Yes, Commander."

Qiu exited the vehicle with his rifle and his radio, and it was with relief that he watched the Mercedes zoom away through the streets in pursuit of the pickup truck. He was alone again, in the dark, in the night, unseen. Away from Li.

He was convinced that the man was becoming unhinged. His decision-making skills were severely compromised, rendering him a dangerously inept field commander. Rage and bitterness had left the man incapable of rationally proceeding through a mission. If Li completed this mission successfully, it would be a miracle of chance. If Qiu made it through this mission without earning a court-martial from Zhao Li, he would do his best to avoid the man for the rest of his life.

He stepped silently through the night to the hotel. There appeared to have been no change, and he assumed the American agents were still asleep. Of course, he had no intention of shooting them dead in cold blood. But if they appeared to be endangering his mission in any way...

His wristwatch told him it wasn't eleven o'clock yet. Finding a comfortable spot in the brush near the parking lot with a good view of the hotel, he settled in for a long night's watch.

A FEW HOURS' SLEEP had to suffice. At 1:00 a.m. they arrived at the Hujan Kalantan wharf. The dock was small and rickety, decaying under the mercilessly corrosive effect of the sea. The boats tied to it were nearly all battered, well-used fishing vessels. There were several decrepit shacks at the wharf side, as well as a single parked delivery truck, once emblazoned with bright red Malaysian characters and a huge green fish, now faded and peeling.

Bolan and Jiahua had been there in the afternoon and arranged to rent a motorboat from an aging, stooped fisherman whose hovel was at the far end of the wharf. They knocked on the salt-stained wood door, and the old man let them in. The soldier, through Jiahua, questioned the old man about any unusual activity on the dock that evening. The old man spoke for a full two minutes before the woman translated.

"One of the fishing boats has been especially active all night. He says it is not unusual activity, per se, because this has happened before on occasion. The owner of this particular boat gets hired to help bring some type of cargo in from another boat that it meets somewhere out in the gulf. Such cargo transfers always happen at night. The old man thinks it is drugs."

"He hasn't seen the Helms yacht, then?" Bolan asked.

Jiahua and the old man spoke again. "He says it has been years since any boat that might be a wealthy man's yacht has been docked here. They must be planning to transfer the plastique to this fisherman's boat out at sea, then bring it in. Maybe Helms is worried about bringing his ship inside Malaysian waters."

The old man pointed excitedly and spoke in hushed tones. Bolan needed no translator this time. They all watched silently out the old man's window as a group of five fishermen crossed the wharf and boarded one of the old vessels. They maneuvered away from the dock without a word. When they were well away from the dock, the engines came to life and a light appeared on the craft. It headed out to sea.

Bolan and Jiahua ran to the old man's motorboat, started it and were moving into the South China Sea waters within minutes. The motor sputtered as it churned the ocean, but it seemed to have been well-maintained. The sea was smooth, swelling and relaxing gently beneath them. High banks of clouds were floating south, leaving the sky clear. They kept a good distance but didn't lose sight of the light from the fishing boat as it moved almost due north.

Half an hour out of Hujan Kalantan, the fishing boat stopped, and Bolan quickly killed the engine on the motorboat. He and Jiahua grabbed the oars and began rowing in its direction.

They heard another engine, and the lights from a ship appeared from the northwest and homed in on it. As it pulled alongside the fishing craft, Bolan made out a Hatteras 58 Long Range Cruiser, a full-displacement yacht capable of carrying the large amounts of fuel needed for long operation, illuminated on all sides as if it were spotlit. The fishing vessel looked gray and dead next to it.

There were shouts and high levels of activity on both the vessels.

"They're loading the fishing boat," Jiahua said.

"Let's get closer." Bolan began pulling again on the oars.

They moved within a few hundred yards. The soldier stripped to the swimming suit he wore under his clothing and eased into the water. Jiahua handed him a rubber bag with a strap, which contained the Beretta and two more of the CIA-supplied AN-M14 hand grenades.

"Good luck," she said.

Bolan headed in the direction of the fishing vessel with steady, quiet strokes. By the time he reached the boat, the transfer was wrapping up. There were closing shouts from the two ships in Malay and English, and the yacht rumbled away from the fishing vessel. The soldier paddled to the wooden ladder that dangled on the side of the vessel and dragged himself dripping from the gulf water. He hung for several minutes, waiting for the Mafia yacht to get out of easy earshot. He withdrew the silenced Beretta from the bag.

He was wishing for a darker, cloudier night as he ascended the ladder and peered onto the deck of the vessel. Five men were on board. One was on the bridge, starting the engine, which was rumbling below the surface. Another two were on the opposite side of the vessel, starboard, drawing in the anchor. Two more were unseen, probably below decks. Bolan saw his chance and took it, sliding over the rail onto the vessel and stepping quickly across the open deck. When he was flat against the wall beneath the bridge, he was invisible to the three men. He waited there for a heartbeat, then opened the door next to him. The companionway leading below was lit with a dim light.

Bolan stepped into the stairwell and glanced below. No one was in sight. He descended into the boat quickly, finding himself in a small cell that opened into a large, open area where fish were deposited through an opening in the deck above. The stench of fish, powerful on deck, seemed to create an almost visible fog in the confined space. Bolan heard movement in the cargo compartment as he reached the bottom of the stairs. He stepped through the doorway and leveled the Beretta at the two men.

"Not a sound."

The two fisherman had been busy securing the ropes around a large pile of plain cardboard boxes. They were both armed with Type 56 assault rifles, but the weapons were leaning against the boxes and were out of easy reach. The fishermen raised their arms and glanced about furtively.

"Open those boxes."

They made small, helpless gestures with their hands and shoulders. They didn't know what he was saying.

Bolan pointed at the pile of boxes and gestured with his fingers. "Open it!"

They figured it out. One of them bent slowly, watching Bolan closely as he did so, and began pulling one of the boxes from under the ropes. Bolan nodded. The fisherman ripped at the heavy strapping tape that sealed the box's seams and was able to get it open with no little effort. He lifted the lid of the box. The fisherman glanced at his companion nervously.

"Take it out." Bolan gestured again, and the fisherman lifted out the contents of the box. It was a heavy plastic bag, but the contents didn't look solid. He gestured again, and the man tore a hole in the plastic. He poured out some of the contents.

Sand.

The fishermen looked at each other, confused.

"Another." Bolan gestured again. The fisherman pulled out another box and opened the bag inside. He poured out more sand. No explosives.

Bolan recalled suddenly the dilapidated fish-delivery truck sitting next to the wharf. He recalled the old man who rented them the motorboat talking about the level of activity on the suspicious boat all night.

There was a creak behind him. The Executioner turned just in time to glimpse a figure slinking down the companionway. He fired into the shadow. The slight retort was followed by a grunt and the toppling of a body. By that time the other two had grabbed their Chinese Type 56s. Bolan fired a second bullet, and a second man died. The third man was a half second too slow. The gun was almost aimed by the time Bolan fired the Beretta the third time. The man slumped against the wall and slid to the deck slowly. The door at the top of the companionway was slammed shut and bolted.

Bolan raced to the door and shouldered it, but it held. He sent three blasts from the Beretta into the door latch, then slammed his shoulder into it again. It popped open, and he stepped onto the deck, firing at the first movement he glimpsed—a figure darting around the front of the bridge.

The soldier didn't pursue, but jumped quickly up the steps to the bridge, and as its interior came into sight, he saw the boat captain peering down the muzzle of a double-barreled shotgun. Bolan ducked, and where his head had been the rail was blown away by the short-range blasts as the barrels went off one after the other. Then he stepped up to the cabin again and fired through the open door. The captain dropped the shotgun and grabbed his gut, bending over. Bolan seized him by the collar and flung him over the shattered railing. The man smashed face and knees first into the deck, then lay there writhing in pain.

There was only one man left on board to be concerned with.

But there was also the rumble of the returning yacht.

It was still several hundred yards away, but was at full throttle and made an impressive sight barreling through the water at top speed, creating a tremendous wake.

The retort of a Type 56 brought him back to the fishing boat. The metal roof over the bridge took the round and buckled and the glass miraculously held. Bolan ducked to the floor of the bridge before the second blast was fired. This time the window took it fully and exploded over him.

He hadn't yet located the gunner, but knew he was somewhere toward the fore of the vessel. Now the clear skies were an asset rather than a disadvantage to the soldier. Leaning out the door at floor level he could make out the dark silhouette of the man standing behind the bulk of the winch machinery. The gunner fired again, and the door swung wildly under the blast. Bolan ducked inside, letting the door slam shut, and moved to the other side of the bridge. The view to the front of the vessel was more obstructed, but Bolan hoped that meant the gunman wouldn't be able to get as clear a shot at him. Maybe wouldn't even see him. He rested his elbows on the floor, aimed the Beretta carefully and fired. The gunman staggered into the open, and the 93-R spoke again, sending the man backward over the ship railing.

The Executioner jumped to his feet, searching for the Mafia yacht, and his worst fear was instantly realized: the vessel had homed in on the motorboat, and Jiahua was running for her life. Lights were blazing from the front of the huge craft, and the woman was like a trapped antelope in the spotlight of a hunter's helicopter. She was swerving, jogging, making the best use possible of the better maneuverability of the tiny motorboat, but the simple fact was that the yacht was bigger, stronger and faster. It was going to get her.

Bolan revved the engine of the fishing vessel, and it began churning the water in the direction of the chase, but its engines were hardly built for speed, so it chugged after the yacht at an agonizingly slow pace. He locked the helm in place and jumped out of the bridge to the deck, grabbing the Type 56 from the dead fisherman and running to the front of the vessel. The chance of his doing Jiahua any good at this distance was slim.

The motorboat veered, spraying water, a sharp turn that almost stalled it out, and the yacht pulled an impressive turn that was almost as agile. The retort of gunfire echoed across the sea. Bolan glimpsed a figure clinging to a low railing on the nose of the yacht and firing an automatic handgun at Jiahua. The Executioner lined up his shot, a highly improbable one even for him. But all he needed to do was cause a distraction. The submachine gun barked a half-dozen times, and he hit the front end of the yacht with most of the rounds.

It worked. The Mafia gunman jumped to his feet, turning his attention to the new threat. He was yelling and pointing. The yacht slowed in response and turned in the direction of the fishing vessel. Bolan sighted the man carefully, adjusted for an imperfection he had perceived in the aim of the Type 56 and fired another six rounds. The gunman danced on the nose of the yacht and flopped into the sea. The soldier aimed next at the dark windows of the yachts' upper cabin. They shattered and disintegrated, and Bolan glimpsed figures retreating below decks. Without anyone at the wheel, the yacht roared past the fishing vessel and out into the ocean, the noise of it diminishing rapidly.

The motorboat chugged alongside the fishing vessel. "Belasko?"

"Yeah."

"Let's blow this thing and get out of here."

"They're a step ahead of us. This ship's loaded with bogus cargo. Boxes of sand."

"Oh, shit! Then the plastique might still be on the damned yacht!"

"I doubt it. The yacht must have arrived earlier than we were told it would. I think it was already unloaded and is en route to Ompang overland. But we can't take that chance. We'll have to destroy the yacht. Here it comes."

Control had been regained on the Mafia yacht, and the white bulk of the ship was approaching the fishing vessel from directly behind. No guns were in sight, but the lights aboard had been cut; only the spotlights remained on and they would soon be flooding the deck of the fishing vessel.

"Stay here. I'll join you shortly." He ran to the rear of the vessel and onto a platform a foot above the deck. It took him scant seconds to blast out the spotlights. The yacht rushed to a halt, churning up seawater.

Bolan sprinted to the front of the boat again and scrambled quickly over the side, landing heavily in the motorboat.

"Drop me off at the back of the yacht," he said. "After that, if the yacht goes after you, use the fishing boat to protect yourself. They won't be able to maneuver fast enough around it."

Jiahua gave the motor gas, and it roared to life. They arced around the front of the fishing boat, traveled along its length within a foot of its hull, then hugged the yacht in the same fashion, invisible to those inside, though the roar of the motor had to have filled the yacht's interior. Bolan plunged into the gulf water just before they swung around the rear, and Jiahua continued her lap around the other side of the yacht.

Bolan swam to the rear ladder with one hand, the other keeping the Type 56 above water. He grabbed hold just before the yacht's engines roared to life again, and it sped around the port side of the fishing boat after Jiahua. He climbed onto the rear deck and hid behind the molding of the yacht's body. He heard no voices and hoped all eyes would be on the fishing vessel—where they may have assumed Bolan was—and the motorboat.

He stepped into the rear aft deck and moved quietly across the outdoor carpet to the door to the cabin. The small, square window showed only darkness inside, but somebody was steering the craft. After a moment he was able to discern their shapes moving against the glowing control panels and estimated only two men were inside. He opened the door and leveled his weapon at them.

"Where is the shipment of plastique?"

He couldn't see their faces, but he could make out their outlines well enough. The man on the left moved his hand in the direction of the control panel.

"Don't do it." He brought the muzzle of the Type 56 directly into the man's face.

Bolan couldn't see that face. But he heard the sneer.

"Fuck you," the hood said, making a grab at the control panel. Maybe he was going for a gun or maybe just to sound an alarm. Bolan didn't care. He fired several rounds into his head and chest, then felt the snick of a rifle bolt as the barrel prodded his side.

"Stop right there, pal."

A third man must have seen Bolan enter the cabin, and had followed him in. But Bolan sidestepped smoothly, brushing aside the barrel of the weapon and feeling the burning heat as it blasted into the wall. The Type 56 swept in a wide circle and shot a half-dozen times into the man with the rifle, stopping again only after it had turned back to the yacht pilot. But the man had already made his move. He'd assumed he would have plenty of time to bring to bear the Browning pistol he had tucked in his belt. He didn't, and he realized it in his final instant, making a whimpering noise that might have been a plea for mercy. Then the assault rifle in the soldier's grip spoke several more times, and the pilot's life abruptly ended.

The Executioner killed the engine, then stole quietly below decks and quickly ascertained that the yacht was now devoid of life save for himself. It didn't take him much longer to search it thoroughly, stem to stern.

He turned on all the lights again and waved to the distant motorboat. Jiahua approached warily at first, then convinced herself it was him and came alongside the yacht.

"Mafia guys?"

"Dead. And no explosives. Tie up the old man's boat for towing. We're taking the yacht back."

"Then what?"

"Then I think we'll find that the delivery truck that was parked at the wharf when we left is now missing. I have a feeling it's carrying the shipment we're looking for."

"Then why'd they go to all the great lengths to get us out here?"

"Another trap. They keep setting up bait, and we keep taking it."

"Luckily we've managed to slip off the hook every time."

Bolan nodded. "So far."

9

The Mercedes followed the pickup truck northwest out of Hujan Kalantan on the main highway, but it soon veered west on a narrow dirt road that led into the jungle. Precipitation the forest had experienced that afternoon gave the surface of the road a thin top layer of mud.

Zhao Li maintained a distance of two miles between himself and the pickup truck and kept the Mercedes' headlights off. In the jungle, in the middle of the night, on a deserted road, the pickup would know from one glimpse it was being followed. Driving with parking lights at high speed required a high level of concentration that was almost impossible to maintain for long. But the road into the jungle seemed endless, and the pickup kept going.

Li complained repeatedly about the incompetence of Men Qiu. In addition, his own two agents, he decided, were a couple of muttering yes-men, agreeing with whatever he said. He didn't know which was worse.

The pickup disappeared.

The commander hit the gas. He'd lost the pickup for minutes at a time when the jungle became dense around him or he let it get too far ahead. This time he'd become self-involved and had lost valuable time. He squinted into the darkness, yanking the steering wheel into turns that came upon him almost too fast to react to. He hit an open stretch and floored it, then went back into the jungle again with its

long, sweeping turns and sudden right angles. Then a hair-
pin curve appeared out of the blackness. Li knew he was
going too fast to take it. Slamming on the brakes, he felt the
tires scooping up handfuls of surface muck, and when he
twisted the steering wheel the car ignored him, continuing
to move straight. A wall of ferns closed around the car like
a massive leafy maw, and the front end dipped into a de-
pression in the ground.

Li screeched in frustration and slammed the gear shift
into Reverse. The wheels whined, but the car remained motionless for a moment, then suddenly shot backward into the
road.

The transmission had difficulty swallowing the vicious
shift into Drive, but managed it with a lurch, and the
Mercedes tore forward through the jungle. Now the headlights went on, and Li shouted to his agents to keep their
eyes open for the pickup.

They saw it just minutes later, parked at a small Malay
hut in a field that opened up in a clearing in the jungle. The
Mercedes came to a halt on the road, and the Chinese agents
approached the hut with drawn weapons. Li got out of the
car when his men waved the all-clear.

"Nobody home. They must have seen us and ran off into
the forest," Yuan Mei said.

"This doesn't exactly look like a compound for
CLAAC," Li said harshly. He cut the rope and tore back the
canvas cover on the pickup's cargo and lifted out a canvas-
wrapped block. The contents were heavy yet almost malle-
able. He cut the canvas wrapping.

Sand sprinkled out onto his shoes.

THE AMERICAN AGENTS had been gone from the wharf only
half an hour when Men Qiu, hiding in the shadows at the far
end of the dock, heard men approaching. They were Ma-

lays, obviously trying to remain undetected in the night. They whispered fiercely to one another, crept from building to building and waited in the shadows for a minute when they reached the dock. Then they ran for the old fish-delivery van, climbed in, started it up and rumbled off into the village.

The truth was now obvious. The explosives were hidden in the van. CLAAC was a step ahead of the Chinese and two steps ahead of the Americans. Men Qiu waited with growing apprehension as his comrades failed to check in.

When Zhao Li finally called in, Qiu reported quickly and heard Li's anger transmitted through the radio. The pursuit of the pickup truck, as Qiu had by now guessed, had proved to be a ruse, a waste of time. It was all Qiu's fault, Li ranted. They were on their way back now.

Qiu wasn't looking forward to their return.

BOLAN ANCHORED the yacht a couple of hundred yards out from the Hujan Kalantan wharf and instructed Jiahua to start the motorboat.

"What are you going to do?"

"Sink it."

"Do we have time for this?"

"It'll delay us only a couple of extra minutes, and I don't want the Mafia getting their hands on it again."

Jiahua looked as though she might be ready to argue the point, but her expression changed to one of resignation. Climbing into the motorboat she revved the engine and loosened the line.

Bolan climbed below with the assault rifle and pointed at the floor, estimating where the fuel lines would run and hoping to avoid them. He blasted the floor with a half-dozen rounds, and water began seeping in immediately, but not fast enough to suit him. Another blast turned the seep into a rush of water. He climbed to the top of the steps, and already the water in the compartment was eight inches deep. Satisfied, he climbed into the motorboat, and Jiahua gave it gas. Bolan glanced back a few minutes later, and the yacht was nearly half-submerged. A lot of Mafia drug money would be spent replacing that craft. By the time they were lashing the motorboat to the wharf, the yacht had disappeared beneath the surface of the sea.

The old man came out, yawning, when he heard the sound of his motorboat returning.

Bolan had already determined the fish truck was gone from the wharf.

"How long ago did that truck leave?"

Jiahua translated quickly.

The man nodded and spoke, and the woman looked grim.

"Thirty minutes or less after we put to sea. They've got a pretty good head start."

They sprinted to the Suburban, which was parked at the hotel, and headed out of town minutes later.

"There's just one likely route between Hujan Kalantan and Ompang," Jiahua said, rattling the map in her hands.

"We'll have to take it and assume the truck will, as well."

"And if it doesn't?"

"If it doesn't, it'll be slowed by whatever alternative route it does take," Bolan replied. "We'll hopefully get to Ompang before it and be able to set up an ambush—if we can find the entrance to the city it will take."

"That's a long shot."

"I know."

The highway grew straighter, and Bolan stepped on the gas, sending the vehicle flying down the highway at speeds that definitely exceeded the manufacturer's recommendations and Malay regulations. But no one was on hand to enforce either, and they were unmolested as the land leveled out and the highway became straight and narrow. They could see for several miles ahead at some points. As far as they could tell, they were the only ones on the road.

Approximately two hours and fifty minutes after leaving Hujan Kalantan, they spotted lights ahead. They gained on the vehicle quickly and realized it wasn't a truck. They easily passed it, a Mercedes 450 SL, traveling at about fifty miles per hour, and Bolan attempted to assess the occupants. Darkened windows and the darkness of the night prevented him.

Only two minutes later they spotted the lights of another vehicle. Bolan slowed as they came up behind and pulled alongside it. It was moving at forty miles per hour at best, and appeared to be struggling to even meet that speed. The side panel displayed a familiar faded green fish. A young Chinese man was at the wheel.

"Damn, I hope this is it," Jiahua said almost under her breath.

"We'll soon find out."

Bolan honked his horn several times, and the truck driver looked at him curiously. The soldier pulled the Suburban in front of the vehicle and pointed out the window, making it clear he wanted the truck to pull over.

"Be prepared in case they open fire."

"Belasko, I think we're barking up the wrong tree."

Bolan maneuvered the Suburban to keep it in front of the truck and decreased his speed, causing the other vehicle to suddenly ride up on his rear end and slam on its brakes. The headlights flashed in his back window, and the horn sounded belligerently. Bolan braked harder and veered when the vehicle tried to pass. The rattling panel truck was no match for the maneuverability of the Suburban. It honked stridently, then withdrew almost a car length and barreled forward with such a burst of speed as it could muster. The panel truck collided with the right rear corner of the Suburban, but as soon as the truck fell back again, Bolan slowed further.

"This is getting us nowhere fast," Jiahua complained.

The rear window exploded. Bolan glanced into the right side-view mirror and saw a dark figure extended from the passenger side of the truck with a machine gun.

"Get down."

Jiahua curled into a fetal ball in the seat. The roof was peppered with bullets, and Bolan swerved to the opposite side of the highway, braking suddenly. The truck shot in front of the vehicle.

"Let's shoot out the tires."

The CIA agent sat up again and opened her window, pulling out her handgun as Bolan neatly tucked the Suburban behind the truck, so close the driver couldn't see them in his own side mirrors. Nor could the machine-gun-toting passenger.

The rear door to the truck started to go up.

"Shoot the tires."

Jiahua leaned out the window while Bolan pulled back a dozen feet and into the middle of the highway, straddling the dividing line and giving the woman a clear shot at the right rear tires. Her shots rang out quickly, and the tire shredded. Instantly the truck began swerving wildly, barely under the control of the driver. Bolan pulled in close behind it again. The rear door was up, and the two occupants of the truck's shipping compartment were clinging to the sides, suddenly in fear of tumbling out.

One managed to drop to his knees, and for a second or two was stable enough to bring his handgun into play, squinting into Bolan's headlights. The soldier already had the Desert Eagle out the side window, and he fired left-handed. The blast went wildly above the gunman's head into the ceiling of the truck. The gunman crouched lower and fired into the highway, attempting to find enough purchase to direct the stream of bullets into the Suburban. Bolan swerved the vehicle to match the slowing, dizzy movements of the truck, and for a moment made for himself an easy shot. He took it. The gunman flopped facefirst out of the truck.

The truck was braking quickly, and Bolan veered to the right again to give himself another clear shot of the interior. The Desert Eagle boomed, and the other hardman never had a chance. The .44 round tore out a good portion of his chest and punched him to the floor of the truck.

The Suburban screeched to a halt, and Bolan jumped out. "Get behind the wheel and stay down."

He sprinted quickly to the truck as it halted and jumped into the rear, waiting for the sounds of feet landing on the rocky shoulder of the road on the passenger side, then the steps running around to the rear. The rifle barrel appeared around the side of the truck, pointing at the Suburban. Bolan grabbed the barrel, yanking it skyward. The gunner uttered a word of surprise in Mandarin, but it was cut off and turned into a grunt when the soldier leaned around the corner and fired the Desert Eagle into the man from less than two feet away. He actually became momentarily airborne, and when his shoulders and neck crunched into the rocks, he was dead. By the time his legs and lower torso had flopped to the earth and were still, the Executioner had jumped to the ground himself and was racing around the driver's side.

The driver was stepping out of the cab, opening fire with a shotgun, but the blast was a panicky first reaction. He might have hit Bolan with the second barrel, but he never got the chance. The Desert Eagle roared again and took off most of the top of his skull. The shotgun slammed into the pavement and blasted into the empty night.

Bolan stepped up to the truck cab and determined no more hardmen were waiting inside. He jogged to the back, waving to Jiahua to assure her the situation was safe, and jumped in the rear of the truck. It had, indeed, been used to ship fish, as the rotten stench attested. But he quickly determined that the boxed contents, roped very securely to the floor, weren't its usual cargo.

Upon seeing Bolan's wave, Jiahua pulled the vehicle next to the truck. "Keep it in gear and be ready to take off."

There was a distant retort; one of the taillights on the truck shattered. Bolan sprang to a crouch next to their vehicle and glanced down the road. A car had cruised to a halt a couple of hundred yards away, lights off, barely visible in the night.

"Kill the lights."

"Now what?" Jiahua asked.

"That Mercedes we passed a few miles before the truck. I thought they looked suspicious." He assessed the situation and developed a new strategy. "Have you got anything with a timed detonation?"

"I have one M-68."

"That'll do. Where?"

Jiahua told him to look in her other pack. Bolan found the grenade, boxed in foam.

"Be ready to get out of here fast."

He raced across the open space between the Suburban and the panel truck and hopped inside the delivery truck. A few more shots were fired, but they seemed to be generally directed, and he heard one of the bullets bounce off the road many feet away. Operating by touch in the blackness, he tucked the grenade under one of the ropes, tight against the highly explosive cargo. It would take maybe two seconds for the miniature thermal power supply in the M 68 to generate the charge needed to activate the electric detonator. Then, without an impact to set it off, the grenade would wait another seven seconds. That meant, in total, Bolan had nine seconds after activation to get away from the grenade and the truckload of high explosives.

He was about to activate the grenade, then realized he couldn't see the undamaged left brake light from the Suburban.

"Put the car in Drive."

"I'll be a sitting duck!" Jiahua shouted back.

"Do it."

He saw the red of the left brake light come on as brilliant as a beacon in the empty, black night, and simultaneously heard the transmission being slammed into gear. Almost at once there were more pops from a distant rifle, and at least one of the bullets impacted into the rear of the vehicle.

Bolan activated the grenade and launched himself from the rear of the truck, an inexorable nine-second countdown beginning in his head.

He jumped into the open door of the Suburban and felt it accelerate at once, tires squealing. Then he turned around, watching out the now-glassless back end. The distant Mercedes had done nothing for a moment, then, without lights, it proceeded in their direction.

"Stop the car."

"You crazy?"

The Mercedes was about to pass the panel truck. "Do it."

The Suburban halted, its single operating brake light like a flare in the night.

The Mercedes slowed and paused next to the cab of the truck. *Three seconds.*

"Now go." *Two seconds.*

Jiahua slammed her foot on the accelerator without further encouragement, and they shot forward. *One second.* The Mercedes seemed to be watching them. It cautiously moved forward, slowly, just a foot or two.

The truck separated at the seams, and white light erupted from inside as if a star had gone nova within its panels. The panels seemed for a brief moment to have dismantled themselves perfectly into their original sheet-metal components, but then they bent and curled like burning parchment and flew away. The truck cab filled with white fire that overflowed out the windows for a fraction of a second before the gas tank ignited and reduced the cab to flying shrapnel. The Mercedes was idling away from the explosion as if it didn't see it or care about it, then the torrents of white fire caught it and rushed through it like water. When its gas tank caught fire its back end flew into the air and the entire vehicle disappeared in the blinding light.

When they stopped the Suburban and looked back, the inferno had already died to a small collection of cool orange flames. The knee-high twisted metal ruins evidenced no clue to the truck and car that had been there just seconds before.

They continued on to Ompang.

10

Men Qiu slipped out of the car with his new rifle and started up the incline at the side of the highway, feeling prickly weeds tearing at his legs through his trousers. He reached the top of the incline and descended the other side as far as possible without blocking communication from the portable radio he carried.

"I'm over," he stated quietly into the radio. A moment later he heard the ringing of shots from the car. They would try to drive the Americans off or at least hem them in and keep them from spotting him until he was in position.

He walked along the slanted edge of the berm until he could see the truck ahead about fifteen yards. The American was inside the vehicle, investigating the contents, apparently. Qiu knelt in the weeds and said quietly into his handset, "I am in position."

"Take them out the moment you are ready," Li commanded.

Qiu pocketed the handset and carefully aimed the L-96 A-1 sniper rifle purchased two days earlier from a Chinese black-market contact. He was in love with the olive green weapon, the finest piece of equipment he had ever used. It was a British weapon, firing a 7.62 mm round. He brought the highly precise scope to his eye and took aim at the rear of the truck, ready to get the American man when he emerged. But he jumped out of the darkened truck too quickly, diving into the car instantly, and the big vehicle was screeching away.

"I did not have a chance to get them. They have been frightened away," he reported.

"You should have fired more quickly!" Li said bitterly.

"Yes, Commander."

He was about to descend as Li halted near the truck, but it was then that the Americans began to act strangely. Their car stopped suddenly. Qiu assumed they were about to get out and start firing on the Chinese car again. He didn't wait to ask for instructions but began running along the far side of the berm. He would get in position and take out the Americans from the side while they were shooting at Zhao Li and the others.

A moment later a wall of sound and gravel collided with him, and he found himself crashing into the earth, rolling through the weeds that clawed at his face and head, while the debris fell around him and his ears tried to cope with the impossible volume of the sudden thunder.

He didn't exactly lose consciousness, but he lay in the weeds, his head and body rattling, unable to see or hear, his senses overloaded.

Minutes later he staggered to his feet, bleeding and bruised, and made his way unsteadily over the berm. The only light was from a couple of small, smoldering flames, one of which licked at the blackened body of Zhao Li.

JIAHUA MOVED to the balcony, a story above the street, and felt lifetimes away from the world she had been immersed in just eight hours before. The morning was late to the people of Ompang, but the woman had just risen. Her body felt bruised and sore, but cleaner and better rested than it had in days. The sun felt luxurious on her skin, warm and comforting. The scene below—the movement of the people in the streets, passing through a small market, involved in their own daily routines—radiated peaceful, small-town predictability.

She felt her partner moving about in the room behind her, and he stepped onto the balcony with her. He stood next to her, scanning the city, and she knew he wasn't seeing it in the same way she was. No romanticizing for Belasko. But that made him the absolute professional he was. She sighed.

"This morning we start the rounds of the neighborhood hangouts. Mix with the locals."

Jiahua assessed him carefully, shading her eyes from the morning sun with her hand as if in a salute. "You won't pass for a local."

"You will. I'll keep my mouth shut."

"What'll I be asking about?"

"Anything. This town has to be aware it's hiding a compound of Chinese terrorists. And they have to have local staff. If CLAAC's in Ompang, we'll find them."

"You seem awfully sure of yourself."

"I'm sure we'll find the compound. What I'm worried about is that we won't find it fast enough. Our recent success in stopping their plastique shipments might motivate them to vacate Malaysia prematurely."

"Prematurely?"

"Before we track them down. Come on."

She sighed again, reluctantly leaving her chair on the balcony. So much for her moment of peace.

Bolan had yet to find a town of any size on the planet without its share of establishments that offered whatever the local beverage of choice might be. In Malaysia the beverage was *tuak* mostly, but that didn't matter. That type of establishment remained the same the world over. As would have happened in any other town, the local clientele regarded the strangers with naked distrust when they entered.

It was early. The place had just opened, and only a few patrons were present. But the conversations dropped to mere whispers when Bolan and Jiahua entered. There was no hiding the big American's non-Oriental features. Leaning against a counter casually, he listened to the conversation his companion was having with the owner, trying to catch some of the meaning in the words. He avoided returning the locals' glares.

They had discussed a ruse, pretending to be looking for jobs and saying they had heard there was a big Chinese-run operation in the area that might hire them. They discarded the idea. They were simply too unlikely a couple. The locals would never buy it. They decided instead to try a more aggressive approach.

Jiahua had purchased a glass of the local grog and sauntered with it to the two occupied tables, next to each other in the rear of the small establishment. She sat down boldly among the locals, seven shabby-looking men, one in his late twenties but most in their fifties. They regarded her with frowns, and most studiously avoided her eyes, Bolan was noticing, as if they each found infinite interest in the walls and the scene out the window and found nothing of value whatsoever in what she was saying.

The woman stopped speaking, and Bolan wondered if any of the group was going to even acknowledge that she was there. One of them made the mistake of sipping from his cup, and Jiahua addressed him directly. He shook his head but said nothing. She called to the owner, who looked uncomfortable, then began to draw drinks. He brought over a round for everyone. The men became visibly distressed. They glanced at the drinks as if they were alive, then took fearful peeks in her direction before redirecting their attention to the walls and the window. Jiahua leaned back in her chair, crossing her legs and draping an arm across the back of her chair as if she were more than content to lounge there for a while. She chatted amiably. Bolan thought the entire group was going to shrivel from discomfort before his eyes.

Finally the youngest man leaned forward, putting his jaw on his hand as if to hide the fact he was speaking, and muttered something. One of the older men snapped at him angrily, and the young man sat back again. He was looking hungrily at the fresh drink—none of the drinks Jiahua purchased had been touched—and Bolan caught his eye for a moment. The young man paled and looked out the window deliberately.

The woman rose and tossed some money to the tavern owner.

"They weren't much help," she said as they walked into the street.

"What did the one man say?"

"He told me to get out of town before we were hunted down and exterminated like rats."

"Interesting but not very helpful."

"Next time sit down with me. Relax. Give the impression you're going to be staying for a good while," Jiahua suggested.

They came to a busier spot, twice the size and with a good twenty customers at small, crude tables. The floor was earth, littered with straw, and the counter was made of scrap wood and tree limbs nailed together into a reasonably serviceable piece of furniture. The countertop was well polished, for all its crudeness. Jiahua purchased them each a drink, which they sipped conservatively as they checked out the clientele. Bolan had hoped they might even be able to spot other nonlocals—surely the Chinese and their staff ventured outside their compound occasionally. But so far, he'd seen no one that looked as if he didn't belong in Ompang.

The place had become more or less silent when they entered, but the conversation was beginning again slowly, quietly, and after getting their drinks, even the tavern owner made a special effort to pretend they didn't exist.

"How about that bunch." Bolan indicated a small group of four muddy men in a back table, all in their late thirties and hunched quietly over their drinks.

"Good choice," Jiahua agreed. "Come on."

They marched to the back of the room and pulled chairs from an empty table. The four men looked somewhat bewildered at the sudden company. The woman smiled and spoke easily. Bolan said nothing, but sat with them, his back to the wall. Jiahua called loudly for a round of drinks. The place had gone still again, and all eyes were on them. Bolan watched the unease of the four men growing exponentially. At least one had become red faced and covered with perspiration. They stared at the table because they couldn't look anywhere else without seeing Bolan or Jiahua or the other customers, who were suddenly wondering why they were on speaking terms with the strangers.

The bartender had failed to bring the round, and Jiahua called again boisterously. The server realized that not bringing the drinks was directing more of the attention onto himself, so he took them over as quickly as he was able, then left them alone. The four locals had an extra challenge. Now they couldn't even look at the table because to do so would be to give attention to the drinks the stranger had purchased for them. Jiahua was speaking conversationally in Malay and, failing to get a response, simply kept on talking.

Bolan noticed movement out of the corner of his eye and turned just enough to see a rear door, made of crudely cut plywood painted brown, open enough for a pair of eyes to peer out. He almost started to his feet before realizing it was only a youth, maybe fifteen or sixteen years old. He evinced amazement at Cello. Then he saw Bolan watching him and drew a lusty grin. The door shut.

"Getting anywhere?"

"Not yet," she answered, but smiled as if she were among friends. The effect of English being spoken was like a current of electricity running through the place. The tavern customers seemed to perk up in their seats altogether, and a buzz filled the place and died away.

Jiahua remarked on this to the man she was sitting next to and laughed shortly. The man, Bolan thought, was going to burst into tears if she didn't leave him alone.

There was movement again, this time to the front. A young man in one of the front tables bolted suddenly from his seat and out the open front door.

"Catch that?"

"Yeah," the woman replied, then nodded to the front door and said something to her companion and laughed again. She drank a hearty quaff from her cup—or at least appeared to—and clicked her friend's mug with her own, urging him to drink up. The front doorway was filled with another figure.

A small man crossed the establishment, stopping before the table. Bolan determined the gun under his arm in a frayed holster was an ancient pistol.

"Leave, please," he said in English.

"Have we done something wrong?"

"Leave, please."

"We just stopped by to have a few drinks with our friends," Jiahua said quickly, too fast for the man to understand. Then she whispered something to her red-faced drinking companion and laughed again.

The red-faced man had taken all he could handle. When the woman touched his shoulder affectionately, he jumped suddenly to his feet, shouting something angrily, still without removing his gaze from the tabletop. He spun in place and marched out the door.

"I guess we're not welcome," Jiahua commented.

"Leave, please!" the armed man said.

The place was obviously not going to be yielding the required information. They left. It was after noon, and the streets were starting to bustle with lunchtime activity. They ate lunch from a small cart selling rice and curry and were looking for another likely spot to get information. The people of Ompang were giving them a wide berth as they walked the streets, but Bolan felt someone brush against him.

"Follow me, please."

A short figure walked past and disappeared into an alley. Bolan recognized him as the youth who had been watching them in the bar. Waiting for an opportune moment when no one was looking, they ducked into the narrow passage after him. They found themselves between two wooden buildings, which led to a small yard enclosed by trees and forest undergrowth. A couple of chickens pecked in the scraggly grass.

The youth was lounging on a rear porch of one of the houses, grinning widely. "Hello, pretty lady."

Bolan looked around carefully. He couldn't see far into either of the houses. Anybody might be in there listening.

"My name is Kin, and I will help you, lady."

"How come you speak English?" Jiahua asked him.

"My uncle is rich and has a TV. I learned to talk English from the TV. And from school."

"You must be smart to learn to speak English just by watching TV."

The youth's grin widened. "Yeah."

"How can you help us?"

"I can tell you where the Chinese people are staying. A whole bunch of them. They're what you're looking for, right?"

"Yes."

"Big place they got. Lots of Chinese there. Lots of cars and stuff."

"Where is it?"

"Nah. You gotta pay, pretty lady."

"Okay. We'll pay. How much do you want?"

"Not cash. You. One hour."

Jiahua said nothing for a moment. "I don't think so."

"Come on. Half an hour."

"Sorry." She turned to leave.

"She's your woman. If you want to know where Chinese are, you tell her what to do!" Kin said to Bolan.

"Sorry, it's not going to happen."

The kid came after them. "Okay, okay. I'll take money."

Jiahua stopped and put several coins into Kin's flattened hand. He gaped at the amount for a moment, obviously more than he'd expected, and then pocketed it quickly.

"This way."

He turned to the rear of the little yard and took them into the rain forest. The town disappeared behind them, and the foliage grew thick. The air became heavy and humid, stagnated by the abundant plant life that buffered and cushioned any breeze that might have stirred the jungle. For all its wildness, there was little in the way of animal life moving about in the undergrowth. Bolan remained on guard, suspicious of Kin.

The path became more crowded with weeds and grass, and the brush closed in as the village was left behind them by a half an hour. The youth pointed to a small pair of hill peaks in the distance, covered with thinner jungle.

He took them across a stream, and any trace of a trail was gone. But they were heading directly for the twin hills in the distance. The march lasted a full hour. Then the jungle stopped at a road, a broken concrete stretch, and started again on the other side.

"This is the road to the Chinese place," Kin explained, whispering suddenly, as they waited in the greenery. "This is the easy way to get there. But it is the way the Chinese take to get there. And there are cars on it all the time. Day and night. And one time they saw me on their road and fired a gun at me. But I ran away into the jungle. Now I never let them see me on their road."

"You are a smart kid," Jiahua said.

"How far from here?" Bolan asked.

"Quarter mile straight ahead, no more."

"Good. We'll take it from here."

Kin shrugged. "Okay, okay. What do you people wanna go there for anyway?"

"I'm sure you'll be quiet about this once you get back to town," Jiahua said, handing the kid a few more coins.

"You bet, lady. Maybe when you're back in town, I will buy you dinner, if your man will let you go out?"

Kin went back the way they had come through the jungle. They waited for fifteen minutes, until they were sure he wasn't hanging around. Then Bolan stepped cautiously toward the road and listened in both directions; the blacktop was swallowed by the rain forest about twenty yards on either side. A vehicle wouldn't be able to hide beneath the quiet hush of the forest. He signaled and they crossed the road quickly, entering the forest on the other side. Bolan heard a car approaching and waved Jiahua ahead. He sank low into the foliage, hidden, and took up watch on the road.

At that moment he noticed the footprints. The ground had been damp in the jungle and they had left clear, wet footprints on the concrete road. In the humid air, despite the heat, the prints were drying slowly. It wouldn't take a trained tracker to ascertain that people had very recently crossed the road into the jungle in the direction of the two hills.

Nothing could be done about it now. The car had almost arrived. He watched it, a late-model Hyundai, windows dark, so there was no way to see who was behind the wheel. It crossed in front of Bolan at a hurried pace. The footprints went unseen.

He turned back to the jungle, and within twenty minutes he and Jiahua started crawling up a steep incline, the rich, black rain-forest soil coming away in their hands as they clawed at the weeds for support. Bolan was the first to reach the top of the hill, and from a low outcropping set in the hillside he found a good view of the compound in the valley below.

The compound was nearly surrounded by the jungle-covered hills, good cover for the operations within. Kin had told him the locals called the place Siah Canyon, but it wasn't a true, river-formed canyon, just a long valley almost completely surrounded by the steep jungle hills. It looked as if it might have been a ranch or a farm at one time, with a low series of old buildings set against the base of the hill. Across the open area of the valley were buildings, tents and a training field of sorts. A dozen soldiers were on the firing range. Several trained in hand-to-hand combat. Many were eating or performing maintenance chores on a caravan of all-terrain vehicles and automobiles. Almost directly below the lookout point, which was on the southern mountain wall, was a wide new building with the appearance of a hangar. A runway crossed in front of it. The valley and the compound were at least one mile from end to end.

Underneath the distant northern wall was what CLAAC most wanted to hide, the reason they had built their compound in such a remote location.

It was a roofless structure, and from their vantage point above it, looked like a maze for a mouse in a scientist's laboratory. But there were people inside—soldiers running the maze with a great deal more intelligence and grim purpose than any lab rodent. There seemed to be control rooms, and in these other soldiers were dressed in white smocks and played the role of the victims of the attack. There were security posts, with soldiers dressed in red playing the role of the guards. There was a large open room near the rear of the maze, and here more white-dressed workers were being held at gunpoint for the exercise.

The soldiers were in fatigues or army greens, and most were quietly holding their captors while a small group hand-trucked in several heavy boxes to the large rear room, where a man in black was busily directing their placement around a wide wooden barrel.

Bolan felt a pit of cold in his gut as he watched the men march through their paces, watching the man in black string together the heavy boxes.

"What the hell is it supposed to be?" Jiahua asked.

"A nuclear reactor," Bolan replied.

11

They spent an hour at the vantage point with their field glasses, observing the CLAAC strike team run through its drills.

The team went first through what appeared to be its standard drill. The team broke into the reactor, secured the staff, planted the explosives and fled.

A roofed platform some five yards tall was situated directly before the replica reactor, and two men stood directing the drill. One came into view several times, and they recognized him as Thomas Comas. The other man was Chinese, gaunt, dressed in black. He barked orders into his megaphone and conferred with Comas often. They assumed he was Kao Lung.

After the first run-through, Lung ordered his attack squad into a small building to wait, hidden from the reactor, and set a large brigade of Malaysians and CLAAC members to work on the replica. The walls were all independent, on corner supports that allowed them to be moved easily from place to place. Within minutes the interior of the replicated reactor facility had been entirely reconfigured. The control rooms had been moved from one side to another. A new pattern of security patrols was in place. More "scientists" in white were placed in the core control area and fewer in the front control area. Then the CLAAC strike team was brought out of its holding room and Lung started the clock again. They stormed the place, assessing the situation at each step and responding with a predetermined sequence of maneuvers. The changes didn't phase the team, which secured the building in five minutes.

Comas saw something he didn't like. Some mistake had been made. He explained it to Lung, who left the tower and stormed into the replica facility, screaming at the captain of the attack force. Whatever the slipup was, it had been so minor Bolan had been unable to detect it from his vantage point.

The soldier was watching the proceedings with a mixture of appreciation and dread. Lung and Comas had indeed created a dynamic, refined attack squad, ready for a multitude of mission variables. Lung's momentary dissatisfaction notwithstanding, his force was polished and prepared.

Lung retreated and had his attack force again sequestered. The configuration was once more changed, under Comas's direction, and now the fake guards were given weapons of an odd shape. The field glasses revealed them to be paint guns. More guards were added, twice as many as during the first run-through, and were stationed throughout the compound. Some were hidden—under stairwells, in closets. Behind a wall. The CLAAC strike team came out of its room with its own paint-ball arms. Lung was looking at his watch, and his voice was clear over the sudden stillness. This was some sort of a final run-through. Bolan looked at his own watch and started a countdown when he saw Lung's raised hand fall.

The CLAAC strike team raced from its starting point in the direction of the replicated reactor facility, the team splitting into four groups. Two attackers in a team to the far right circled far around to the left, another two to the right and a single primary-strike team attacked via the front. The last team held up as backup. The frontal attack took the guards stationed at the front of the building. One of the Chinese soldiers stepped quickly into the front door of the building, as if sensing the guard hidden behind the wall about to sound a general alarm, and eliminated him with a splatter of red paint. The man playing the guard fell to the ground with a huge stain on his forehead. If the gun had been real, his forehead would simply have been missing. The frontal team secured the entrance to the facility and waved in the backup team to hold it. The frontal team penetrated the facility with its hand truck full of explosives.

Meanwhile, the left-flank team rigged a window, presumably to bypass the alarm system planted there, smashed the glass and shot the guard that stepped into the room. More guards followed, but the intruders were faster. The attacking guards were covered in red paint. The one paintball round the reactor defense managed to fire hit the wall several feet away from the intruders.

The right-flank team had more difficulty. They were spotted through the window of one of the facility's rooms and were fired upon by the guards. Bolan saw the eager determination in the manner of the guards. This was as much an exercise for them as for the attackers. They were doing their damnedest to ensure the attackers' failure.

The right-flank team dived for cover, and one of their members crawled to the window, took out one of the guards with a well-placed shot and lobbed in a grenade. The room erupted in smoke. The two right-flankers didn't wait for it to clear, but headed for a window next door and broke inside. Bolan wondered what the smoke grenades were supposed to represent. Would the real attack force be carrying tear gas? Or something more deadly? Because when the smoke from the fake bomb cleared moments later, the guards in the room were all sitting down, defeated. A tear-gas grenade would have sent them fleeing into the hallways.

The right-flank team scented out and eradicated two guards before meeting in the hall with the left-flank team. They proceeded through the corridor, securing each room, marking the walls with red chalk to indicate to their companions in the frontal team that they had already passed. The four soldiers eluded discovery by a squad of guards at the reactor core area, who were on alert—Lung's attackers were operating under the assumption that the alarm system would be activated almost immediately upon their entrance to the facility, despite their efforts to the contrary. Lung was without a doubt preparing for a worst-case scenario.

The guards were gassed, then attacked through the clouds and eliminated. Bolan watched the looks of surprise on their faces as they were covered with red paint stains suddenly, as if out of nowhere. They sat down. Four more guards out of the picture.

The frontal-assault team, now behind the combined right- and left-flank teams, joined them and together they proceeded into the reactor core.

Meanwhile, behind them the rear guard was making its way forward. The "dead" guards rose again and began stalking them. The rear guard began picking them off with precision and care, tricking the guards into revealing their positions, hemming them in, gunning them down, yet again, mercilessly.

The large primary-assault team blew the door with firecrackers designed to simulate charges. The door held. They tried another explosive type. The door held. Bolan wondered what explosives were being simulated. Then they approached with a handful of clay and plated it with a firecracker, obviously designed to simulate plastique. They ran into the hall, and the door blew, swinging open. Guards rushed through, a half dozen of them. They fired wildly into the hallway, and the Chinese returned fire calmly and began covering the guards with paint-ball stains. The guards weren't dropping. Three, then four times each guard was hit before he was considered dead. It took the Chinese twenty seconds to finally wipe them all out. But their marksmanship was superb. The six guards were dead. The CLAAC strike team hadn't been hit.

They entered the reactor core area with their hand truck, placed it against the simulated core containment and one of them turned it on. A red light glowed on top. The team began a hasty retreat. Firecracker "bombs" were detonated behind them—the team was sealing off each room as they proceeded out, minimizing the chances of anyone getting to the reactor core before it was detonated by their plastic explosives.

One of the Chinese took a bullet. His arm was nicked by one of the red paint balls. Surely it wouldn't have been a killing wound. But the man stopped and sat down where he had been hit. The rest of the team met up with their rear guard and fought their way out to the front, then out of the building and into the trees.

Bolan looked at his watch—3:23. In less than three and a half minutes, the CLAAC strike team had beaten unreasonable and unrealistic odds and performed their mission. In real life the human resistance in sheer numbers wouldn't be half or even a fourth of the numbers Lung and Comas had staged. And Bolan doubted the People's Republic kept highly skilled marksmen on guard duty at their reactors—the resistance would be at best as skilled as the resistance staged at the replica. If Lung had accurately simulated the problems the strike force would meet in terms of getting past the alarm systems and physical structure of the facility, then the force was almost assured of success.

"Do you think Comas can guide them well enough into a reactor's interior?" Jiahua asked fearfully. "Do you think they have enough plastique to really destroy a reactor's defenses?''

Bolan nodded. "Ever see the event trees used to predict potential nuclear loss-of-coolant accident paths? The simplified versions include five potential causes of a loss-of-coolant accident. Simple stuff like power failure, broken pipes and failure of the containment building. Or something more complex, like the failure of the emergency core-cooling system or fission-product-removal failure.''

He looked at her. "I have a feeling Lung wants to take out the containment. That would cause the most significant and long-term failure. But one of those loads of plastique would pretty easily destroy the cooling-pipe system and the primary and redundant electrical systems, as well.''

Jiahua didn't respond. Bolan had to admit he was impressed by the training that had been undertaken. Lung knew what he was doing. These men were good at their jobs.

But their job, successfully executed, might result in the deaths of tens of thousands or hundreds of thousands of people.

He watched Lung berating the single CLAAC strike-team member who had been shot by a paint ball. The man hung his head in shame.

Comas and Lung conferred for several minutes, after which Lung ordered the team sequestered again. The sun was high. There was lots of daylight left, more opportunity to hone his team to an even higher caliber of expertise.

Bolan had seen enough.

THE MALAYSIAN CAPTAIN, Nan Cohr, approached the tower with two Chinese captains. Lung had learned to like Nan Cohr; in fact, he trusted him as far as he trusted any Malaysian. Cohr had demonstrated a kind of ruthless loyalty to Lung—purchased, of course, but nonetheless genuine. Lung had put him in charge of the other Malaysians in the compound guard. They seemed to look up to him.

"What is it?" Lung asked, taking the ladder down to the ground.

"Mr. Lung, I've had reports from a couple of my men who were in town this afternoon. There was a woman there with an American man. She spoke Malay, as well as Mandarin and English. She was asking if anybody knew the location of a Chinese-run compound in the area. They were playing some intimidation games with the people. They are pretty determined to find the place."

"Our American, with his accomplice! They have come to us."

"It would appear so."

"What became of them?"

"After stirring up things at a couple of taverns, they were last seen talking to a kid in town, Kin Nun. That was early this afternoon."

"Who is this Kin Nun? Has he worked for us?"

"No, sir. He's just a boy."

"But is it possible he knows about the compound."

"It's possible, sir. Let's face it. Just about everyone in Ompang knows about the compound, even if they do not know what happens here."

Lung nodded determinedly. "All right, all right. Cohr, I want the guard doubled tonight. Do we have enough men for that?"

"I'll get the men."

"Good." He addressed one of his Chinese captains. "Chai Ling, I want the posting of CLAAC members doubled after dark also. But right now I want twelve teams. Ling, you organize it with Nan Cohr. I want one of each of our CLAAC members on each team. Cohr, I want four of your men on each team. Get into town. Track down that kid. Make him tell you where our American friends are, then make sure he doesn't tell anybody else. Get our American friends. Track them down. I don't care who you have to pay off or how many townspeople you have to eradicate to do it. I want them found and I want them found today. Understand?"

"Yes, sir," Ling said.

"Dead or alive, Mr. Lung?" Nan Cohr asked.

Lung considered this a moment, then said quietly, as if he were musing to himself, "Alive, preferably, but I'm not fanatical about it."

BOLAN AND JIAHUA marched quickly back through the rain forest to Ompang, carrying in their minds the image of the crude wooden replica of the nuclear reactor on the CLAAC compound, and the utter precision with which CLAAC infiltrated it.

As they approached the city, they left the trail, skirting the two small homes that backed up to the rain forest. They marched through the foliage and out of the brush onto the main road of the town. They began heading in the direction of the small hotel and spotted a familiar figure heading in their direction on a rusty bicycle.

"Hey, you made it back!" Kin shouted breathlessly. "I thought I was going to have to come looking for you. You realize you got lost from the path?"

Bolan said nothing. Jiahua complimented him on his bike.

"Just bought it. Cost me a fifth of what you paid me. Been down by the market. You guys are being looked for, you know that?"

"By who?"

"Chinese. And guys I know from Ompang. They are working together. They came into town just a while ago and began looking all around for you. They'll find you, too. You're easy to spot.''

Bolan led them off the main street to a smaller dirt road that ran between the small houses. They paused against the wall of one of the houses and scouted the area ahead. It was clear for the time being.

"How many groups?"

"Lots. They came in a bunch of different cars and trucks. You must be important.''

"Well, we expected our little displays this morning to garner some attention," Jiahua said.

"Yes. We can't go back to the hotel. We can't risk driving the car, either. We'd be sitting ducks. We'll have to stay on foot as of now.''

"What's the plan, by the way, from this point on?''

Bolan glanced at the kid, who was riding in the narrow lane in front of them, out of earshot. "I've got to get inside the compound and find out if they have more plastique stashed there. And if so, destroy it. They look like they're ready to launch their campaign any time now. I have to make sure it doesn't proceed.''

"You?"

"Yeah, me. I want you to get out of this town and to a secure phone. Contact your CIA friends in Kuala Lumpur and get some reinforcements.''

"And from that point?''

"Depends on how well I do tonight. That base has got to be destroyed. Even if I fail miserably, I don't think the CIA will touch the situation, officially. But my people will send in a team to clean it up if I can't manage it.''

"How do you expect to manage it in the first place? Alone against that army?''

"We'll see. If we move quickly, we might get the rest of the hardware out of the Suburban before CLAAC's search-

and-destroy teams get to it. Think we can get to the hotel fast enough without being seen?''

Jiahua nodded at Kin. "He'll help us."

Bolan thought about it quickly, then agreed. He hated involving the kid in this affair. Who knew how much danger he was putting him in?

They called the boy over and, for another coin from Jiahua's supply, he agreed to ride ahead of them and give a yell if he saw any of the search parties, thus allowing Bolan and the woman to get back to the Suburban at a quick pace without hiding behind each and every building. They started off in a jog down the narrow lane, glimpsing the main road through the ramshackle buildings to their left. The small town of Ompang grew gradually more metropolitan, by Malaysian standards, with each mile.

Twice the kid yelled loudly in a singsong voice, and Bolan and Jiahua retreated to the cover of one of the buildings. Both times they heard the sound of approaching vehicles and, from their hiding places, watched cars drive by slowly on the main road, each time with a Chinese at the wheel.

Ten minutes later they were back at the Suburban. It was parked next to the large white building that served as a small hotel for the town. Eventually CLAAC would trace their whereabouts to this place. Apparently they hadn't yet done so. From a nearby building they watched the scene for a few anxious minutes before deciding to take the chance of approaching the vehicle.

"Get out of here, Kin," Bolan growled. "For your own good, you never saw us."

"Very welcome," the youth said, and sped off on his new bicycle.

They quickly approached the vehicle, parked behind the building, Bolan with his hand inside the zipper front of his sweatshirt, gripping the handle of the Desert Eagle. It was midafternoon and the hotel was quiet. The nearby clumps of trees and brush were like pieces of the rain forest that had broken away. Jiahua quickly opened the glassless rear end of the Suburban. The CIA-supplied hardware was in a locked storage compartment.

Bolan's gaze was drawn to a nearby tree. He wasn't sure why, perhaps some hunter's sixth sense for seeking out prey. The Desert Eagle appeared in his hand, and he leveled it.

Jiahua looked up with surprise and drew her own gun.

"Come out," Bolan said levelly.

From behind the tree, a hand appeared holding the barrel of a British sharpshooter's rifle, an Accuracy International Model PM, also known as an L-96 A-1. "Don't shoot me, Mr. Belasko." The tone was matter-of-fact, not pleading. A young Chinese man stepped from behind the tree.

"Identify yourself."

"Men Qiu, Chinese secret service. We had better get out of here. CLAAC is combing the city."

"We know." The Desert Eagle's aim traveled to the man's skull as he approached with careful steps.

"You're going to have to take the chance that I'm telling the truth."

"I don't have to do anything. I can just leave you right here."

Qiu's eyes traveled to the muzzle of the powerful handgun. The sound of an approaching vehicle drew their attention.

"Could be CLAAC," he stated.

"Jiahua, you ready?"

"Yeah," she said. "Let's get out of here."

Bolan gestured with the Desert Eagle, and Qiu turned quickly. They jogged into the nearby trees, separating themselves from the Suburban. The soldier glanced back, saw the open area was still empty and led the three of them across another bare stretch into the thin rain forest on the edge of the town. Another glance back revealed a Toyota station wagon pulling to stop. Three Malaysians walked inside the hotel, but the Chinese man at the wheel spotted the gray nose of the Suburban tucked in its hiding place behind the building. He rolled the Toyota forward another fifteen feet, where he could see the vehicle clearly. Once he identified the vehicle, he jumped out of the station wagon, shouting into a handheld radio.

One of the Malaysians raced out the front door of the hotel to see what the excitement was about. The Chinese man yelled, "Search the place! Every room! They were here!"

The Malaysian rushed back inside. The Chinese driver continued yelling into the radio. Bolan urged his companions through the woods. A minute and a half later they came to another dirt road, deserted, with more rain forest beyond. The Executioner stopped long enough to listen. Nothing. The forest between them and the hotel now blanketed the sound of any activity there.

They stepped into the road quietly, but as if they had tripped an alarm they instantly heard a car approaching at high speed. Bolan sank to one knee and gave Jiahua a shove, sending her across the road, and began to fire the Desert Eagle the instant the car appeared. His shots were high, on the off chance an innocent local was driving the vehicle. But a Chinese was standing up out of the sunroof and had an Uzi submachine gun leveled on Jiahua the instant the vehicle swung into view. The shots from the .44 pistol failed to distract him from his target.

Bolan aimed his third shot, and the gunner's shoulder exploded, sending his upper torso flopping onto the roof of the car. He wasn't dead, but the soldier had to neutralize the driver. The .44 Magnum round burst through the windshield like a rock through a picture window and smashed into the driver's face.

The car veered wildly just as the passenger's forearm appeared out the side window and fired a small handgun. With the car's erratic motion, it was a near-impossible shot, but Bolan heard the crackle of the air where it passed him. He blasted at the corner of the car as it roared headlong into the rain forest. The car's passenger slumped sideways into the lap of the dead driver, and the vehicle crashed solidly into a tree trunk, sending the wounded man in the sunroof flying to the ground, where he lay still.

Another car was seconds behind it, far enough back that it screeched to a halt before it could meet a similar fate. Bolan fired once, and the windshield changed from transparent to opaque. There was a blast of rifle fire at his shoulder, and the front tire popped. Men Qiu's eyes were glassy and bright, and he moved the rifle ever so slightly and fired again. The other tire blew.

Bolan blasted once again and knew he'd hit the passenger. The car sped into a desperate turnaround in the narrow street, front tires flapping, sending its rear tires into the muddy jungle edge, where they proceeded to spin furiously, leaving the vehicle motionless. The soldier aimed for the driver, who was angrily shoving at the corpse next to him as he wrestled to get the car moving. The driver glanced at him in terror at that moment, and a gaping pit appeared where his right eye had been.

Now it was time for the two Malaysians in the back seat to panic. They sank below the windows, and the door on the other side of the car opened. They crawled out, and one of them appeared over the trunk, firing a small pistol once. Bolan answered in kind, and the Malaysian was sent sprawling.

Qiu was shooting through the car at the final survivor, who was opening the driver's door and dragging out the corpse. There were brief glimpses of him as he crawled into the driver's seat, keeping low, and tried to maneuver the car away from the bloody scene. He hit the gas, and the vehicle lurched forward a few feet, front tire flapping, and as soon as two inches of his head appeared over the back of the seat, Bolan and Qiu fired their weapons simultaneously. The two inches of head were blown away.

There was another gunshot, and a bullet seared the air inches from the Executioner. The man who had sprawled out of the sunroof was still alive. He had flopped onto his belly and brought his Uzi into play, and the recoil had nearly knocked it out of his weakening grip. He was aiming it again when shots began to echo from the barrel of Jiahua's Colt All American. Standing over him, not five feet away, she emptied her clip into his back.

"One cold bastard," she breathed, addressing no one in particular.

They raced into the rain forest.

12

By late afternoon they had traveled in a circle almost a mile wide and were headed back in the direction of the village. Ompang was quiet by the time they got there. Bolan didn't trust the silence, however, and they waited on the edge of the foliage, watching the lack of activity. They were at a point west of where they had fled the village. No houses were visible, only the road and the jungle on the opposite edge of an open area. Their immediate goal was to cross to safety. Such a crossing meant being in the open for more than two hundred yards. If any type of patrol was to come by, they would be pursued again.

They had listened to the search parties crashing around in the fringes of the jungle for a couple of hours, never venturing very far into the foliage, warned off by the collection of dead men at the forest's edge. Eventually the search parties must have realized searching at the forest edges was without purpose and they retreated, ostensibly back to the Siah Canyon compound. But there were no guarantees. There was every chance the group of gunmen would be heading back to Ompang and had established a watch perimeter.

Bolan stood motionless in a mass of ferns, field glasses to his eyes, moving almost imperceptibly. He was scanning every visible square foot of jungle for signs of movement and saw none. Three times people passed them on the road, villagers who didn't rouse his suspicions.

He satisfied himself that the jungle around their locale was empty of watching eyes. Jiahua and Qiu looked up anxiously when he stepped back from the road to where they waited. Before he could speak, they heard a pain-filled, plaintive wail from the east. It was a cry of unmitigated sorrow. Bolan stepped to his watch point again and scanned the road as the sounds grew slowly nearer.

First he saw a group of women, stepping down the middle of the road, heads hung, children silent and wide-eyed in their arms.

The wailing grew louder, a single woman's voice, and next he saw a mule plod into view in the middle of the muddy road, pulling behind it a crude wooden cart with one piece of cargo—a bloody, bruised body. The wails came from a woman who walked behind the cart and clung to the dead foot of the corpse, her body bent over from trying to avoid the rickety wooden wheels but unwilling to let go. She looked at the dead figure curiously, almost as if she were unable to believe he was really dead, then raised her eyes and cried out, long and sorrowfully. Several other women surrounded her, sharing her grief, eyes on the skies or on the road.

It wasn't until the sad parade passed directly in front of Bolan that he was able to make out the features of the corpse. It was the youth from the restaurant, who had shown them the route to Siah Canyon. He studied Kin's body—bruised ankles and wrists, black eyes, swollen and blackened abdomen, a dozen small cuts placed strategically about his body. The boy had been tortured.

He stepped away from the road into the deep green forest life.

"What's going on?" Jiahua asked.

"Funeral. I think when it passes we'll be able to cross."

"Good."

"You're coming with us, Men Qiu."

"Yes. I think we can mutually benefit one another."

"If you've got any grudges to settle, better do so now."

"It would not be professional for me to contemplate revenge."

Bolan ignored the comment's implications and stepped back to the road, watching the last of the procession disappear around the bend into the jungle. He waited for the wails of the boy's mourner to fade, scanning the jungle with all senses. Taking the chance that no watch had moved into place during the commotion of the procession, he signaled to the others and they stepped out into the open. Between Bolan's non-Asian features and their packs and hardware, there was no way to hide the fact they weren't locals. They started quickly across the open space.

The mosquitoes were buzzing in the hot, humid sunshine. The road was a dry crust on top, but a muddy slurry where it had been walked on or wheeled over. They crossed it, stepping in existing footsteps, and wiped their feet hastily in the grass, then began crossing the open section of tall grass, which was when they heard the approach of a motorcycle. It was the harsh, thin whine of a midsized engine at high revs and coming fast.

They broke into a run and headed into the forest as they heard the buzz of the bike come into the open. Bolan gestured, and Qiu aimed the MP at the vehicle as it swung onto the road. If the rider gave any indication he had spotted them, the Executioner would give the order to neutralize him. He watched the mirrored glass of the helmet as the bike swung by, looking for any telltale motions that would indicate the rider was glancing in their direction. He didn't see any, and the man was allowed to live.

"We should have shot him," Jiahua said. "He very well could have seen us."

"I don't think he did. And if I'd killed him, CLAAC would know we were back in town. We might as well retain whatever level of surprise we have."

"But where to now?" Qiu asked.

"We located a path that goes to the south wall of the CLAAC compound, which is located in a spot the locals call Siah Canyon. We were up there earlier today and staked it out."

"We're going back there?"

"I've been relegated to other duties," Jiahua said.

"I'm going back," Bolan stated. "I want to get in there as quickly as possible and shut them down however I can. If they have a stash of plastic explosives inside already—a stash anywhere near as large as those we've seen—then they have everything they need to launch their attack. Their strike force is as trained as it needs to be."

"You cannot go in there alone," Qiu said.

"I have to go in there alone. The place is packed with well-armed soldiers, Malaysians and CLAAC terrorists. I've got to be able to sneak in undetected and locate that supply of explosives."

"I cannot allow you to go in alone. This is an affair of the People's Republic of China and is not under the jurisdiction of the United States."

"It came under my jurisdiction when I was nearly gunned down by your comrades on U.S. soil last week. Your secret service almost killed Chiang before we could use him to track down CLAAC. As it is, we barely were able to halt the shipments of explosives that have been coming in over the past twenty-four hours."

"We were on the verge of halting that shipment ourselves. You stupid American, my men were the ones you blew up at the truck last night!"

"Why'd they try to kill me?"

"I told you, this is not your jurisdiction!"

"Look around, Qiu. You're not in the PRC anymore. This isn't your country any more than it is mine. If you're suggesting those of us without 'jurisdiction' go home, then let's call on the Malaysian government to send in its own agents to take care of the situation."

"The truth is that this problem came from China and its aims are directed at China, and all you've done is hinder our efforts!"

"Wrong. The truth is that the Chinese almost erased the only lead they had for locating CLAAC, and would be sitting around without a clue as to the group's location if I hadn't kept you from getting at Chiang. And CLAAC has the staff and the hardware for at least three simultaneous nuclear-facility attacks and would have been supplied with enough plastique for all three of those attacks if we hadn't been able to track them down and destroy two shipments. I've seen their strike force, Qiu. It's well-trained and itching for action. And if Kao Lung and Hank Chiang are frustrated enough, they may very well spring that force on one of the PRC's reactors soon. Maybe tonight. Have you considered that Daya Bay is only a fifteen-hundred-mile flight from where we're standing?"

Qiu was momentarily stunned. "Daya Bay...?"

"Yes."

"Daya Bay is the most technologically advanced nuclear station on the planet. And I'm sure one of the most carefully guarded."

"No matter what security measures have been put in place, they won't be enough. Not if I've assessed Lung's capabilities accurately. He's ready to meet whatever defenses Daya Bay or any other nuclear station throws at him. And if Daya Bay goes, Hong Kong, the entire Kowloon Peninsula becomes wasteland."

Qiu rested a hand against a small tree and stared at the earth. Perhaps he was imagining the Kowloon Peninsula made unlivable.

"In the face of such a possibility, I think our goal should be first and foremost to cut down CLAAC where they stand. We'll worry about international jurisdictions later," Bolan pressed.

"I suppose you're right."

"Good. I'm going into the compound tonight, without either of you. I want you to get reinforcements."

"Where in Malaysia are we going to find reinforcements?" Jiahua asked.

"You're agents for two of the most powerful countries on the planet. Make use of those resources somehow. I don't care how you do it. But I'm only going to be able to do so much damage on my own. My plan is to wipe out the major cogs in the machine. But we'll need a backup force to come in and strip the machine completely."

"How many men are stationed at this compound?" Qiu asked.

"A hundred and fifty. Maybe more. About a third or more of which are CLAAC personnel. The rest are locals. That may explain why we've been able to move about town as easily as we have—many or most of the local men are at the compound working. We need a force that can wipe the place out. Mostly we have to make sure we secure the CLAAC members. I don't care about the locals, but the Chinese are going to be carrying around this plan and the expertise they've gained. We can't let a single one of those loose cannons escape to fire itself off later."

"Agreed." Qiu was looking thoughtful, maybe still dwelling on the image of a Daya Bay disaster. Good, Bolan thought. Keep him afraid of the situation, keep him well motivated.

"I think, however, it would be best to start with your government," Qiu added. "Mine will be less than cooperative, especially once they learn of the situation here—with the rest of my team dead."

"All right," Jiahua said. "Let's go. We'll have to hike it out of this town, get to a secure line and contact Washington."

Her look lingered on Bolan just a moment, then he turned and was hiking away from them, into the woods.

It was late afternoon and the hottest part of the day. The sun beat down on the treetops and created a steam oven beneath the rain forest canopy. The perpetual dampness of the forest surrendered enough moisture to raise the humidity level into the ninety percent range. Bolan's back was quickly covered in sweat, and his dark hair became slick. He stopped just long enough to wrap a handkerchief around his head to keep the sweat from running into his eyes. Otherwise, his steady, silent march through the jungle was uninterrupted.

He had left Jiahua and Qiu on the north side of the main road, which ran east-west through the small town of Ompang. He continued north, gradually changing his direction to veer east, toward the path they had traveled earlier. Glancing at his watch, assessing his relative position in the rain forest, then glancing at the level of the sun peaking through the treetops, he calculated his location and guessed he would meet up with the path just after 5:00 p.m.

He found it at 5:04 p.m. and paused in the cover of the woods just long enough to listen. There was no sound around him that wasn't indigenous to a tropical rain forest.

He stepped out onto the path and headed north, now able to proceed in a near-jog with almost no noise whatsoever.

Less than half an hour later he crossed the stream and the path was more or less gone. Then he was in the foliage again, which meant he couldn't hope to proceed with as little noise if he wanted to maintain his pace. On the other hand, his chances of meeting with anyone were significantly reduced.

A late-afternoon shower was in developmental stages, clouds rumbling together in the sky as if coming out of nowhere, and when they finally let loose, it was a relief rather than an inconvenience. The rain was cool, and Bolan could almost feel it absorbing the rest of the moisture from the air as it fell. He marched through it, and within minutes it had stopped, the water soaking into the already sodden jungle floor. Darkness was still a couple of hours away when he started up the hill and came to the lookout rock he and Jiahua had visited earlier in the day.

Activity, as Bolan had feared, had stepped up inside the compound. Malaysian workers were moving rapidly about, carrying large quantities of equipment and matériel. There seemed to be a large garage in the basement of the central building, which the soldier thought was primarily a bunkhouse, and the vehicles were moving in and out of it with loads of gear. Gathered in groups were those Chinese who were not directing the activities of the Malaysians, and several were wandering about the wooden replica nuclear station, studying it as if their lives depended on absorbing the very essence of the structure.

There was little he could do prior to darkness. Bolan watched, trying to ascertain the causes of the activity. It could only mean an imminent attack. His destruction of the two loads of explosives had forced CLAAC's hand. They were preparing to make their attack soon. The following day, maybe even that night. All they needed was transportation. He assumed Chiang and Lung would have taken care of that detail and arranged for aerial transport. But if Bolan could get to that plane, render it inoperable, it would significantly hamper their plans.

QIU LED JIAHUA into the jungle outside the village to the spot where his car was parked. Tucked in a nest of ferns and weeds twenty feet off the dirt road, the Australian-model Ford was invisible until they were nearly upon it. Nevertheless, they spent twenty minutes approaching it and stopping to wait for signs of other life. There was none. Finally they dragged the ferns off the Ford and started it up. The steering column was largely exposed.

"Where'd you learn to steal cars?" Jiahua asked.

Qiu grimaced proudly. "PRC secret service taught me."

They idled through the foliage to the road, waited for signs of other traffic, then turned onto it, heading away from Ompang.

They came to another village within eight miles, and in that time had seen no other vehicles traveling either direction on the Ompang backroad. The most modern-looking building village was a small grocery-convenience chain store. Jiahua went inside.

There was no pay phone, but the owner of the store let her use his business phone to make her call, charging her the equivalent of eleven dollars for the privilege. She didn't feel she had the time to haggle. A moment later she was linked to a small CIA office in Kuala Lumpur.

She explained the situation succinctly to her liaison, then held while the agent tried to get through to Washington. Any action that would require coming in contact with the government of Malaysia had to go through Langley. The minutes dragged by, and she heard nothing but silence from the other end.

The chime rang at the front of the store as another customer entered, and Jiahua stood on her toes to see him over the row of merchandise. It was an old, bent, scrawny man walking with a hand on his back as if it pained him.

The speaker clicked. "Still there?"

"Yes. What can you do for me?"

"We're going to have to work on this one. Can you get back to us in an hour or so?"

"Have you been listening? We don't have an hour. We need some damned backup here."

"I wouldn't hold your breath. We've got to explain this situation to some pretty high-level folks here in Malaysia, who aren't going to be too happy that we've had an intelligence operation on their soil right under their noses. When we're done insulting them, we've got to ask them for help. See why it's risky?"

Jiahua had never met her liaison in Kuala Lumpur, but she hoped she would some day. She'd tell him to his face that she thought he was a complete incompetent.

"How about I try back in half an hour?" she asked.

"Even an hour is pushing it, Jiahua."

She didn't have time to answer him. The old man straightened, becoming much taller than he'd appeared, and leveled a single-barrel shotgun at her.

"Hang up," he said in Malay, and his mouth widened into a grin. "Keep your hands raised, palms to me, moving slowly."

Jiahua replaced the receiver and held up her hands.

He waved with the gun to the door.

"Out."

Jiahua stepped to the door, and her eyes flitted about the road and the front of the small store, but she couldn't find Qiu. She wondered if he had abandoned her.

"Now what?"

"Quiet!" the old man snapped. He stayed several steps behind her. She turned around casually, hands still at shoulder level, and leaned her rear end against Qiu's car.

"We just going to stand here?"

"I said shut your mouth!" The old man glared at her, then craned his neck to see up and down the road.

A car appeared, and the old man relaxed. It came out of a hiding place in the jungle a couple of hundred yards to the east and pulled up next to Qiu's car. The two Malays who got out had Type 56 assault rifles.

"Good job, old man," one of the men said. He pulled a wad of bills out of his pocket and peeled off several for the gunner. "We'll take it from here."

The old man shouldered his shotgun, grabbing at the currency with childish eagerness and heading off onto a path through the trees behind the building.

"Well, you've got me. What're you going to do with me?" Jiahua asked.

"Take you to Lung, what else?" the Malay said. "You've caused him quite a bit of trouble, you and your friend. I don't suppose you want to tell us where he is?"

Jiahua grimaced.

"We might find a way of getting the information out of you," the Malay suggested.

"You might."

He regarded her. "On second thought, I doubt it. Anyway, it's up to Lung. Would you like to wear these for me?" He tossed her a pair of handcuffs.

A cry of surprise and pain came from the woods, and the old man flopped out of the trees, hitting the ground with a thud and lying still. A section of his forehead was smashed in.

The Malay shouted and fell into a squatting firing position. His comrade gurgled deep in his throat at the same instant a retort was heard from within the forest. He fell motionless. The first Malay shouted in alarm and began unloading his rifle into the trees.

Jiahua jumped forward and kicked the weapon's barrel skyward, then snapped her foot into the Malay's stomach. He bent and stumbled forward a few steps, but she grabbed the barrel and yanked it in the direction of his face. He straightened with a fresh grunt of pain. The heel of her palm plowed into his face, but the impact was slightly misjudged and instead of rocketing the fragments of his nose into his brain, killing him instantly, she only managed to smash it flat. He roared, blinded by agony, spinning and flailing for the gun when she snatched it out of his hands. Her next kick smashed his testicles, and he dropped to the ground. She stepped into him and kneed his skull, which twisted with violent suddenness. The snap that came from his neck was as loud as the shot that had killed his companion.

"No, I would not like to wear these for you," Jiahua said harshly to the dead man, tossing the handcuffs at him. Then she started in the direction of the forest, drawing her own gun, only to find Qiu stepping out of the growth.

"You hurt?" he asked.

"No. How about you?" The woman shook her head.

"Sorry I had to leave you with them. I saw them driving up with the old man and knew something was up. I headed for cover, hoping I'd be able to help you out."

The owner of the grocery store had appeared, standing on his stoop and staring down at the dead man. Jiahua found the keys to his car in the dead man's pants pocket.

"What are you doing?" Qiu asked.

"I'm hoping we'll be less conspicuous if we're in one of CLAAC's cars."

Qiu looked at the vehicle, then looked at Jiahua. He was thinking that the car might fool an observer from a distance, but once they got close up, despite the boyish cut of her hair it was unlikely the woman could be easily mistaken for male.

"What did your contact say about backup?" he asked.

"My contact said we wait."

"Then we should get rid of both cars," Qiu said. "They probably spotted us by our car. Not many in this part of the country. They knew an unfamiliar one instantly. If we're going to stick around here, then we ought to get both vehicles out of sight."

She opened the trunk of the CLAAC auto and grabbed the first dead man under the shoulders. "Give me a hand."

THE SUN BLAZED above the highest peak, then suddenly dropped below it. Bolan crawled down the hillside below the lookout rock and found the vegetation thinned, then the incline quickly turned into a sheer cliff. But, hidden from the sun, the ridges of the cliff afforded patches of dark cover. It wasn't too early for Bolan to make a move.

He located a coil of 11 mm rope and rappel gear in his backpack and hammered a piton into the rock. He clipped a carabiner, the climber's snap link, to the metal ring in the piton and strung the rope through. Holding both ends of the rope, he stepped over the cliff edge. Bouncing a little, he rappeled down the cliff cautiously, with as little disruption as possible on the rocky, crumbling walls. The rocks he loosened with his feet were small and rolled to a stop at the slight incline that developed near the floor of the cliff.

It would have been ideal for Bolan to have come down directly on top of the building he assumed was the hangar, where the still-theoretical airplane was stored. But he was going on the basis of caution at that stage and remained in the shadow of the crevice, coming down in a bit of bushes at the base of the cliff a hundred yards to the east of the hangar. He moved out of the protective wall of the crevice and into a patch of grass less than waist high. It bordered the concrete runway, which was newly, and crudely, poured. He assumed the locals had put it in, patch after patch, smoothing it out with their shovels and hand trowels. The result was a wavy, uneven stretch of cement that would make for a bumpy takeoff or landing.

The stream of Malaysian laborers had ceased bringing loads into the hangar, and now it was the Chinese who were entering with their packs and their weapons—and they were very heavily armed. Bolan spotted Uzis, the F-88s, even some old Australian F-1 submachine guns. CLAAC had obviously sourced arms down under. The Type 56s, the Chinese AK-47 copies, were omnipresent. The Chinese were milling about the front of the building, and Bolan determined from their aspects that there was indeed a large garage-type door on the front of the building, though he couldn't see the front of the building from his hiding place.

The shadows from the sun had lengthened on the canyon floor, and by the time the light was growing dimmer and traveling up the canyon walls, the convoy from the village was returning. Bolan realized with the arrival of this group that he had underestimated the total number of men stationed at the CLAAC compound. The total had now grown to one seventy-five, maybe even two hundred.

The arrivals pulled their vehicles into the parking area on the far side of the compound, between the reactor replica and the large building Bolan had come to believe was the headquarters and billets for the upper-echelon Chinese. A large four-wheel-drive vehicle pulled away from the rest and came to a stop before the front of the hangar. A gaunt Chinese man in a narrow-cut black outfit stood on the tarmac waiting for the four-wheel-drive's occupants to come to him—Lung.

Bolan dived into a crawl and made his way on hands and knees through the patch of grass to its very edge, hoping to get close enough to Lung to make out the conversation. When he stopped, dangerously near to being exposed, the occupants of the vehicle had reached Lung and were obviously giving some kind of a report. They were too far away. The soldier couldn't hear a word until the man in black started to scream. The fury seemed to come over him suddenly, as if a switch had been activated. The man spoke in Chinese, and he was obviously angry.

The man making the report tried to defend himself, and he waved to the final vehicle, an ancient, tiny Toyota station wagon with the rear door flopping open and several pairs of feet sticking out.

The gaunt man in black walked across the compound stiffly and quickly, and was waving at the makeshift hearse, where a group had gathered to help remove the corpses. He was screaming at them, too, gesturing at the road that led out of the compound. Clearly, he was ordering them to return to the town and resume their search for Bolan and his allies.

The entourage piled into their cars again and left the compound, taking the dead men with them, leaving the gaunt man standing in the middle of the Siah Canyon fuming and watching them depart.

Bolan was sure now that the man in black could only be Kao Lung.

13

Jiahua and Qiu paced the aisles of the grocery store for more than two hours. The owner, a meek man in his fifties, didn't complain about their loitering, though it was clear he was uncomfortable with their presence.

The day was getting long when they heard a vehicle drive by, away from Ompang, moving slowly. Men with assault rifles watched the landscape as they drove past. But the Chinese saw nothing to alarm them in the tiny village, and they didn't pause there.

Minutes later Jiahua and Qiu heard the sound of a vehicle tearing through the jungle, and the same car sped through the village again, heading back to Ompang at a dangerous speed. A minute later they ascertained the reason for its flight—four large, camouflaged Malaysian army troop transports appeared on the road and halted suddenly in front of the small store. The woman and the Chinese agent ran out to them.

"Xiaoliao Jiahua! U.S. CIA," she said to the driver of the first vehicle, and jumped in when one of the rear doors opened for her. "You can call me Jiahua. Let's get that car before it's able to warn the others we're coming!"

The Malaysian captain pointed, and the convoy accelerated again. The condition of the muddy, slick roads was of little consequence to the heavy, four-wheel-drive troop transports, and Jiahua knew they could outrun the auto the CLAAC hardmen were in—if the lead didn't prove too big.

Luck was with them. She spotted the CLAAC car dead ahead, only a hundred yards away, and it was at a stop, trying to recover from a spin in the slick earth. Mud flew from the rear tires as it fishtailed, then bit the road and accelerated quickly. But the Malaysian army driver was accelerating, as well, eating the distance between them.

The captain ordered the third soldier, sharing the back seat with Jiahua and Qiu, to bring the CLAAC car to a halt. The man prepared his rifle, but Qiu raised a hand. "Allow me," he said. He climbed over the soldier to the right-hand rear window and angled his head and shoulders out to sit on the window ledge. He moved with deliberate care, getting a comfortable position with which to use his sniper rifle, then waited for the driver to bring them to within twenty or thirty yards. He needed only one shot. The car's rear windshield developed a hole, and the driver slumped forward on his steering wheel. The car failed to take a curve, and it crashed into a tree.

Jiahua jumped from the military vehicle before it had halted and sprinted into the forest, following the trail of ruined vegetation. She pointed her pistol at the passenger, who had been flung through the windshield and into the tree that had halted the car. But he was just a corpse now. She checked the driver, who was also dead.

"That's that," she called to Qiu. "Let's go clean up Ompang."

QIU CHECKED THE ALLEY in both directions, the sniper rifle held close like a dance partner, pointed straight at the sky. No one had seen them. No one knew they had returned to Ompang.

Jiahua nudged the rickety door with the Colt, which was gripped in her left hand. Wedged neatly under her right arm was the Heckler & Koch MP-5 A-5 submachine gun.

"I want some answers, and I want them right now!" The man's voice from the other side of the door was menacing.

She jimmied the barrel of the Colt in the opening, and the door swung out a half inch more, enough for her to see a CLAAC terrorist throw something across the room. The object was a cup of *tuak,* which broke, the liquid splashing on the walls. The alcohol smell reached her almost instantly.

"I know he's here somewhere. Where is he hidden?" The man was gesturing with his assault rifle, intimidating the occupants of the room.

The tavern clientele, not surprisingly, couldn't supply the man with an answer. They looked fearfully at one another.

"Come here!"

He reached out of Jiahua's line of sight and came back with a young woman in his grip. She gasped and tried to drag her arm out of his hand, but she was tiny and her strength didn't approach his. No woman at all, the CIA agent saw. She was just a girl, maybe thirteen, a server of drinks. The old tavern keeper stepped forward with a cry of alarm, and the assault rifle the CLAAC terrorist held was jabbed into the girl's stomach.

"Stay back. Your daughter, eh, barkeep?"

The tavern owner immediately began begging and bargaining for the life of the girl. Jiahua didn't think she had a chance. The men of the town had no currency CLAAC was interested in.

"If I get the American, I don't shoot the girl. How's that, barkeep? A pretty good bargain, I think. What about the rest of you?"

"Please, please, we honestly don't know where the American is," the tavern owner said. He was stooped, made pitiful in his fear. "We would tell you if we knew. Please don't hurt her."

Jiahua had seen plenty. She let the door close quietly and briefly laid out the floor plan to Qiu. "There are three Chinese that I can see. The one you've got to get first will be directly in your line of fire. He's got the girl held in his left hand. When he notices us, he'll probably turn in our direction and drag the girl in front of him. You'll have to miss her."

Qiu nodded, expressionless.

"Are you sure you can miss her?"

"Positive."

Jiahua paused thoughtfully. "Man, you had better not hit that little girl."

"I won't."

Qiu stepped back and aimed the rifle directly at the door, finger on the trigger, ready to fire, and Jiahua pulled it open quickly. He took in the room in a glance, and it was as the woman had told him: the CLAAC terrorist turned bodily when the door opened, and the young girl was yanked to the side, becoming a shield. Qui adjusted his aim in that split second and fired. By the time the father and his daughter were screaming, the blast had filled the room and the bullet found its mark. The terrorist's head was flung back, a trickling hole in the bridge of the nose, and his grip on the girl loosened.

Qiu's body didn't seem to have moved, but the rifle's aim had to have shifted, because when it spoke again another terrorist on the opposite side of the room tumbled into the wall, clutching his rib cage. The third Chinese stepped forward with his finger on the trigger of his Uzi, but the Colt All American pistol spoke first, and a 9 mm parabellum round caught him in the stomach. The second hit the pectoral, the third the sternum and the heart.

The tavern customers watched the carnage almost insouciantly, except for the father and daughter, who were embracing and sobbing in the corner. Jiahua jumped inside.

"Get out of the way!"

The patrons looked at one another as if they didn't understand her words, though she was speaking perfect Malay.

"Get out of the way!" she repeated.

The tavern door swung open, and a Chinese terrorist burst in firing without aiming his submachine gun. Jiahua fired a round into him, catching him in the thigh and twisting him forty-five degrees. She cut loose with the MP-5 A-5, the bullets tracing a trail neatly up his spine as he sank to the floor, and then into the man entering directly behind him. The second hardman was already falling away from the door when the rounds started stitching his chest and he fell backward into the night.

Outside she heard shouts in Chinese. She ran to the door, jumping over the crouching Malaysians, who were finally doing as they had been told, and peeked through the crack in the doors into the street. CLAAC hardmen were assembling. She poked the nose of the MP-5 A-5 through the door and triggered on the group. They dived for cover, scrambling behind a large foundation of square-cut rock in the street, where a stone animistic symbol and a rough-hewn cross were unlikely partners.

Qiu, meanwhile, fired a barrage of bullets through the back door, just in case anybody was sneaking up from the rear.

There was a quick discussion in the streets, then a Chinese voice called out in English. "Give it up, American! You're surrounded. You're cornered like a rat!"

Jiahua had no intention of being the trapped rat, as she was just then telling the Malaysian army captain over the radio he'd provided her. He answered affirmatively, and in the tavern they heard the sound of the large military troop transports storming in their direction. The Chinese in the square were looking about curiously, having thought they were the only mobile units in town. Three military trucks roared into the small square, and the rifle fire erupting from them was deafening. The Chinese made no attempt to return fire but turned and fled.

Jiahua watched the Chinese tumble to the ground one after another, cut down from behind and from the side, only a few lucky souls somehow finding an enchanted path through the deadly torrent. As soon as they made it safely to the other side of the square and into the village, two of the military vehicles roared off in pursuit.

The square was clear, and Jiahua moved to the back of the tavern. Qiu was aiming out the back door into darkness, where the occasional armed silhouette in the headlights of the fourth military transport made ideal targets. He waited for them, stock-still and watching, snapping his aim onto their forms when they appeared, firing with near-instantaneous response. Soon the terrorists who had planned to break in through the rear of the tavern were lying still or had run in the other direction.

BOLAN BOLTED from the grass, across the open space, and went flat against the outside hangar wall. The sun was gone, and the compound was darkened except for concentrated pools around stark lamps placed about the operations areas of the compound. There was no one in sight; the substantial activity of the afternoon seemed to have abated. He was still at risk of being seen every second he wasn't under cover.

He waited in the shadow for only a second. No alarm was raised. The compound stayed quiet.

He circled into the darkness and tall weeds that provided cover over the back of the hangar. There was no egress, window or door, not so much as an air vent. The building was configured in such a way that its back wall angled into the canyon cliffside, and the west corner actually touched the canyon wall. Bolan tramped through the weeds. Having left his rappeling equipment dangling on the cliffside a dangerous hundred yards behind him, he had nothing to help him get up the cliff. But this spot near the bottom of the wall of rock was particularly jagged. He launched himself on it, grappling for handholds, kicking the loose stone to make nicks his feet could somehow wedge into. When he was six or seven yards off the canyon floor, he was able to climb onto a jutting piece of rock and brace himself against the cliff and the corner of the building. Around the west side of the building there was a pool of light, some twenty yards away, cast by a lamp on a pole. A Chinese guard stood beneath it, scanning the compound. He tucked his rifle under his arm, reached in his pocket and took out a cigarette and lit it slowly. He flicked the match away, watching it glow orange and die in the grass.

Bolan hung motionless, watching the guard, knowing he would be visible in the glow of the light. All the guard had to do was turn.

The guard stood there.

The Executioner inched himself up, the brick corner of the building tearing the flesh of his palm, the cliff wall crumbling under his other hand. Over the course of the next two yards the space between the cliff and the building became narrower. The soldier twisted and wedged his back against the cliff, feet against the corner of the building, and then his hands were free.

He drew the silenced Beretta 93-R, rested it on his lap and, with a lunge, was able to grab his shoelace and drag it out of his shoe. He made a slipknot and tied the pistol to it, putting the other end in his mouth. The gun dangled there as Bolan continued his ascent, ready for quick firing.

He reached a point where the cliff sloped away from the building again and transferred all his weight to the cliff face, fingers struggling to find holds strong enough to support him. But the cliff was getting flatter as he went higher. He grabbed for a small ledge, almost directly over his head and just barely in reach, and started to pull himself up when the rock separated from the wall, as it had only been lodged in mud. Bolan lurched downward and quickly slammed his hand into the hole the torn-away rock had made. His feet, precariously placed at best, lost their hold, but his fingers in the new hole held. He hung on for a moment, supported only by the one hand and unable to maneuver himself. He didn't know how much noise his scramble made, or whether the guard under the light post had heard him and was about to gun him down.

Bolan felt with his toes and came up with impressions where his feet could somehow gain purchase, then transferred his other hand to the hold above him and was able to twist a look to the right to see if the guard had been alerted.

Shoulder against the light post, the guard lowered the cigarette to his side and blew the smoke above him, watching the backlit clouds of smoke disperse into the darkness. He was unaware of an enemy presence.

The Executioner breathed through his teeth, gritted around the shoelace holding the Beretta and craned his neck to assess his position. He was level with the roof of the hangar. Level wasn't good enough—the distance between the cliff and the roof was now so great that Bolan would have to leap to it. He had to get higher. He clawed at the rocky face, hoisting himself on the new impression and feeling for a handhold higher up. The rock had become solid and sloped away from the hangar again. There was no handhold to be found.

Turning to the corner of the hangar again, he examined the distance and his own situation, trying to decide what his chances were of actually making the jump. He would have to leap out almost horizontally in order to grab the brick ledge of the roof, and that leap would have to cross about two yards. He had barely any foothold, hardly enough to hold him where he was, let alone provide the leverage for such a jump.

The ground was now a mass of darkness below him, and distances were hard to judge. But he'd come up a long way. He would probably survive the fall if he missed the roof, but he sure wouldn't be in good shape.

Left hand locked in his one solid hold, Bolan rocked his body back and away from the cliff face, then again back, and he pushed against the rock wall. As the rock under his shoes crumbled to sand, he watched the corner of brick roof flying at his face and extended his arms. His hands reached over the roof and slammed into the foot-wide brick ledge. He hooked his hands and arms on the ledge with all his strength, ignoring the sudden wetness as the bricks scraped the flesh off his hands, ignoring the impact that followed. Then he hung on the side of the building, still.

But only for a half a second. Bolan dragged himself over the ledge and flattened himself against the roof, behind the ledge, and readied the Beretta. He peeked over the ledge, prepared to fire.

But the guard on the light post never detected a sound. He was tossing his cigarette away and strolling away from the hangar.

Bolan examined his hands—scraped but not badly injured—and relaced his shoe, then headed for the large, mushroom-shaped air vent in the middle of the roof toward the front of the hangar.

Inside, the huge fan blades were spinning at a casual pace, and the light shining through from the interior of the hangar was strobing. Bolan grabbed the base of the mushroom-shaped cap and exerted cautious pressure. It refused to budge at first, then scraped against the aluminum base. Once loosened, it was easy to pull the hood off and rest it on the roof. Snaking his arm underneath the whirling, two-foot-wide fan blade and using the well-worn wire cutter in his Leatherman Pocket Multi-Tool, he cut one of the wires leading into the large electric motor. The sound and feel of hot interior air rushing onto his face began to lessen as the fan blade slowed, its momentum keeping it rotating for at least another minute. By the time it came to a halt, he was hearing the voices of the speakers inside the hangar. One of the voices he recognized as being Hank Chiang's.

"You sure we shouldn't put the plastique in the plane?"

"It's safe," said the second voice, which Bolan immediately applied to the dark-clothed, gaunt man. Lung.

"I don't like this, Kao. He could be anywhere."

"My men will find him."

"Your men are looking in town. I'm guaranteeing you there is no way that guy is still in Ompang."

"They'll look outside the town. They'll look everywhere until they find him."

"They have only three hours. By then it won't matter anymore."

"They'll keep looking. Throughout the night. Long past the departure of Fire Hammer. I have sent Hu Lei to tell them we canceled our plans for leaving tomorrow morning. He will inform them that I have decided to wait another few days. They will keep looking and won't dare to come back here until they have found him.''

There was silence. Bolan, peering down through the fan, could see a large section of the floor of the hangar. The interior was dominated by a Lockheed L-188 Electra. The aircraft had a wingspan of just over thirty meters and was powered by four Allison Model 501-D13 turboprops. Bolan knew its top cruising speed was about four hundred miles per hour, and its range could easily be over two thousand miles, even carrying seventy members of CLAAC terrorists. Daya Bay was less than two thousand air miles from their location right now, even if their route swung them out over the South China Sea to avoid a Vietnam fly-over. In fact, much of China was within their flying range, depending on their route and how much weight they carried.

Piles of empty boxes and debris were pushed to the walls, away from the plane. There was no sign of others, and he couldn't yet see Chiang and Lung.

''And have you?''

''Have I what?''

''Changed the plan to depart tomorrow morning?''

''Hang, I would not make such a change without conferring with you first. We are coleaders of this operation.''

Chiang laughed shortly, accusingly.

''But Hu Lei believes I have changed the departure date. If he has any doubts, he will not dare act upon them—I was very angry with him at the time he left. The others will believe him and they will not dare act if they have doubts, for the same reason. And after 1:00 a.m. it will all be irrelevant.''

''We need those men, Kao.''

''Don't you want that bastard dead, Hang? He's seriously compromised our operation. He's cost you nearly a million dollars in lost merchandise. In my judgment it is worth the loss of the men if they stay here and find him.''

Bolan saw a Chinese guard walking along the open front of the hangar. He glanced in and nodded at its interior, in the direction of Chiang's and Lung's voices. Only when he had gone past did Chiang speak again.

''The point is, I don't think they *will* find him.'' Chiang was speaking more softly now. ''He's too damned good. I mean, yeah, let's look at what kind of damage he's done to us, assuming it has been the same individual all along. He's nearly wiped us out, single-handed. He's trained, he's talented. He's not going to have any trouble getting past your bunch of bumbling idiots. And where do you think he's going to head then? Right here, Kao. If he hasn't got this place staked out already.''

''That's the reason for the accelerated schedule.''

''I know. But what I'm saying is, there's no point in leaving those men out there wandering around the village when they could be better used right here.''

''You seem pretty worried, Hang. We've got only three hours.''

''A hell of a lot can happen in three hours,'' Chiang said with a snort. ''Let's go at midnight.''

''The plan is to leave here at one and strike at 5:00 a.m. That's when we know security will be most lax.''

There was a silence that conveyed Chiang's nervous frustration as clearly as anything he might have said.

''You sure we shouldn't put the plastique in the plane?''

''It is safe where it is!''

The voices were getting closer, and Bolan saw the two men pass underneath the exhaust fan. He ran to the front of the roof, watching Chiang and Lung head directly across the open compound. Now was his chance to get down and inside and plant one of his grenades under the fuselage of that plane. Even if the plastic explosives weren't on board, he could gain a lot of time by rendering their air transport unusable.

Wedging himself bodily between the fan blades, feet first, he climbed out underneath the motor in the steel beams of the ceiling support. The hangar was empty but well lit—anyone who happened to walk back and glance up at the ceiling would spot him. He climbed along the beams as fast as possible and shimmied down a girder along the west wall.

Hearing footsteps, he crouched for cover behind a five-foot-tall tool chest and drew the Beretta. Several men—he guessed eight or ten—were marching into the hangar. All were Chinese and well armed. Bolan assumed Chiang had convinced Lung to post a substantial guard on the plane, just in case. Two of the men ascended the back stairs to an elevated steel work area. The rest spread out on the main floor of the hangar on both sides of the Electra.

Bolan went unseen, but his opportunities for an easy kill on the plane were frustrated. He assessed the odds of getting a grenade to the aircraft and then being able to get away unscathed and decided they were slim. There were too many guards in the immediate area. He would have to take care of the plastic explosives first, then he could take his chances on the plane.

The immediate task was to find the explosives. Chiang had more or less told Bolan they weren't in the plane, but had inconveniently neglected to say where they were.

Now the challenge was to get across the wide expanse of the open compound. He was tempted to try a simple, casual walk in the hopes that he would look enough like one of the local Malaysian staff that he would go unchallenged. But he realized there were no Malaysians out tonight. Lung had probably decided they weren't worth the risk this close to the start of the final phase of the operation.

He would have to get across unnoticed, which meant a slower, more careful crossing and wasted time. But he wasn't strapped for time—not yet. One a.m. was the hour Lung and Chiang had more or less decided on as the final phase for the launch of the Fire Hammer. A little less than three hours to go, by Bolan's watch.

He waited for an opportune moment when the guards were looking in the other direction. After they settled into their posts, it was an easy opportunity to come by. They were talking among themselves, and the nearest guards were facing their comrades toward the back of the hangar. Bolan slipped around to the front of the building. The area before him was clear all the way to the other side of the compound, and again he was tempted to make a simple walk across. But he knew that was unwise. He slipped around to the western side of the building.

And he faced the guard under the lamp post. The man had returned to his spot—not a well-chosen one, as the light above him cut down his visibility and made him plainly visible to any intruder. But he was facing the building now, as it happened, and spotted the dark figure against the brick hangar wall instantly. He grabbed the cigarette from between his lips and said something in Mandarin. It was clearly a demand for Bolan to halt.

The Executioner aimed and fired the Beretta, and the guard slumped against the post, sending the circle of light on the ground wobbling. Bolan raced to the man, snatched him under the armpits as he came to a rest in a sitting position and dragged him quickly into the dark grasses against the cliff face. Shoving him deep into the grass, then bolting behind the hangar, he paused to listen. He heard nothing immediately, but that didn't guarantee he hadn't been seen. He raced along the back of the hangar, peered out the other side and bolted for another patch of grass and low vegetation. The farther he went along the back of the compound, the deeper and wilder the growth became.

He circled around the far eastern side of the compound, behind the starting point of the runway, jumped the tiny stream that ran through the valley, then came to the edge of the sprawling replica reactor. He would be plainly visible if he walked along the front wall. To get to the other buildings, he had to pass through the monstrous structure.

14

Bolan easily scaled the wooden wall, which reminded him of a Wild West fort more than anything else, and found himself in an open-air hallway. He turned to his left, having memorized the current configuration of the replica earlier from the lookout point. He passed a darkened room to his right before coming to a corner and turning right again. Ahead was another room to his right and, farther ahead, there should have been another corner, which would cut again to the left and to the front door of the replica facility.

He halted, examining the wall five yards ahead. As difficult as it was to make out the configuration in the nighttime, with all the different layers of shadows, he was sure there was only a blank wall there, with no opening to the right, although the room to the right was where it was supposed to be. Bolan stepped up to the door of the room, listened inside, then stepped into the room with the Beretta at the ready. The room was empty. He quickly left and continued down the hall, finding that the exit hall he'd planned to use was, in fact, closed off. Listening carefully and detecting no sound beyond the wall, he attempted to lift it out of the way, as he'd seen the walls being moved from place to place during the change in exercises earlier.

The wall wouldn't budge, as if it were locked in place.

A light directly above his head came on.

The soldier sprang away from the light source, sprinted down the hall and ducked to the left. He paused at the corner and listened briefly, and noticed a light on a pole just outside the corner of the fortlike walls. Even as he was glancing at it, it came on—and the first light died. Bolan stepped into the door of the room to his left, ascertained it was empty and ran on, past his entrance point and to another hallway to the left leading into the interior of the facility. He checked it—empty. Another light on a pole a half-dozen paces away illuminated and the one behind him went dark.

A blaring air horn from the middle of the compound erupted, shattering the quiet of the night. Bolan heard the instant sounds of activity and voices. Footsteps were approaching the replica. He ducked down the hallway into the middle of the wooden maze. All the lights that had illuminated thus far had been situated outside the replica itself. Maybe by keeping to the middle he could stay hidden in darkness and make a determination as to his next move. Remaining unseen was paramount at the moment.

A voice was shouting from the west side of the compound, and the air horn continued to blare. Bolan recognized the voice as Lung's.

Footsteps and shouts began to spread around the replica, and Bolan knew he was being surrounded. He also knew they wouldn't know where he was if he avoided any of the lights with the motion detectors. He ducked into the first of two hallways to his left and found himself in a large room without other exits. He ran out again, took the second hall and raced along a sharp right followed by a sharp left, his instinct telling him he was heading in the direction of the front exit. If he got there quickly enough, he might be able to fight his way out the front. But he came to a dead end and headed back to the opening of the hallway, dead center of the compound.

It was at that moment that lights went on all over the replica, and Bolan found himself standing in plain sight. Whirling on the observation tower, he drew the Desert Eagle and fired it three times quickly at the face that had appeared in the tower front. The face ducked, but another one appeared. It was Kao Lung, wearing a grim smile.

He shouted into a microphone, and his voice blasted over the compound in place of the air horn. Bolan fired again, twice, but saw Lung duck behind the wall, and the shots punched into the ceiling of the tower room. The first man appeared again with an Uzi and opened fire at the Executioner, who dived behind a compound wall and kept moving once he was out of sight of the gunman.

With the lights on, Bolan was a fish in a barrel. He had to get rid of some of them. He targeted the nearest light pole and blasted the glass dome away. His area of the compound dimmed. He sighted three more within shooting proximity and extinguished them with three rounds from the Desert Eagle.

The wall above Bolan was splintered with several rounds from a rifle, and he glimpsed a figure clinging to an outcropping on the northern incline. The north wall was far less steep than the south, and the Chinese were clambering to its top, giving them an excellent viewpoint for activity below in the replica.

Bolan sprinted down a hall and vaulted to a south wall directly in front of him, grabbing at the top with one arm and holding himself in that position long enough to fire at the hillside. With five quick rounds he took out the gunman and another Chinese next to him. He let go and plummeted just in time to watch the wall where he had been hanging shatter into pieces from the fire coming from the observation tower.

The soldier rolled to his right and was again in a narrow hallway that temporarily protected him from the north and south. He jumped to his feet and shot out two nearby lights, engulfing himself in deep shadow. Peering around the corner, he saw the tower gunner trying to orient his sights in the sudden change in illumination. Bolan reloaded, aimed quickly and fired three times. The man's chest and face became splattered with red, and he slumped out of sight. Lung was nowhere to be seen, but his shouts from the loudspeakers became screams in Mandarin and in English.

"Get more men on that damned hill! I want him taken out right now!"

Bolan ran up the hallway, giving the hill-perched gunners a clear shot but counting on the darkness to hide him, and ducked to the right again, only to find himself in a parallel hallway that still left him exposed from one side or another. Better to be exposed to the tower gunners than the hill. There were by now too many men on the hill for him to control effectively. He jogged down the new hallway, firing at a light ahead and to his left, taking it out just as he was stepping into its field of illumination, and firing a volley of rounds at the gathering shapes on the hill. He watched them scatter but doubted he'd scored any hits, then ducked to the right again and reassessed his situation.

If his sense of direction was correct, he was very near to the simulated reactor containment room. He was in a tiny room, like a vestibule, a pole with a destroyed light standing in it. A few steps to the left opened up the room, and he found himself indeed in the large, open area of the replica reactor.

The crude wooden image was inspiring not so much in what it was but in what it represented. Bolan didn't consider the magnitude of that symbolism now, and he didn't attempt to dwell on the justification behind its existence. He'd run into madmen in the past and knew the futility in trying to understand them and their affinity for murder.

He sighted, fired and took out a light on the opposite side of the open "room," then ran to the massive bulk of the wooden reactor barrel. With its mass to his back he was protected from the gunmen on the hill, and he had a clean, clear shot at the tower. He aimed at the faces framed in the window. One of them had to be Lung. He fired, and both faces dropped from sight. The voice over the loudspeaker continued with renewed fury.

"Stop firing! I repeat—stop firing into the structure. The quarry is behind the reactor! Do not fire at the vicinity of the reactor! Bring the vans to the walls and put gunmen on top. I want every avenue covered."

The soldier detected a hint of panic in Lung's voice and wondered what that had to do with the strange orders not to fire in the vicinity of the reactor. He bent low to the ground and tried to see inside the massive wooden bulk. Finding a gap in the wood that was wide enough, he inserted his arm and withdrew a single narrow cylinder. It was a stick of dynamite. He stretched his hand inside and ran his fingers quickly over the sticks, counting them. He was sure he couldn't reach them all, but he still came up with roughly one hundred.

CLAAC was planning to blow the replica reactor when they were done with it, and perhaps Hank Chiang saw some gleeful parallels in the act of using the crude, bulky explosives to blow up his crude, pretend reactor in the same manner that he would blow the much more sophisticated real item with much more sophisticated explosives.

Bolan understood now the panic he'd detected in Lung's voice. The dynamite in the barrel-shaped structure was sufficient to blast the entire wooden structure to kindling, and such an explosion would smash the observation tower flat. It would take only one wild shot to ignite the dynamite and turn half the compound into a fireball.

The soldier took advantage of his temporary safe harbor. Looking for the loudspeaker, he found two of them wired to the legs of the tower about four feet below the observation room. He blasted the first one with a .44 round from the Desert Eagle, knocking it off the tower. A second round silenced the other.

Bolan, pocketing the stick of dynamite he had grabbed, kept a close eye on the empty tower window as he made quick work of reloading the Desert Eagle. At the first sign of movement he drilled two more rounds into the opening, then stepped around the bulky wooden mass and sighted on shadows flitting across the hill behind him. He fired four shots and knew he'd made at least two good hits. A wave of panic ran through the enemy gunners, and the Chinese were departing the hillside en masse. The shouted orders coming from the tower probably couldn't be heard in the chaos on the hill. Even if the hardmen had heard Lung, Bolan knew it was unlikely they would heed him. And then he spotted one last man on the hill, far to the right and with a clear shot, devoid of the panic gripping the others. The gunner saw the shadow of Bolan just as the Executioner saw his enemy's shadow. They were evenly matched over the distance of the night.

The soldier pivoted, gun arm horizontal, and knew full well he might not be quick enough to pick off the man on the hill. So be it. In that instant he experienced a modicum of admiration for the man, who stood courageous when his fellows fled in terror. Bolan wasn't one to argue the fine line between courage and foolhardiness in battle. He fired and watched the man on the hill crash onto his back following the impact of the big .44 slug.

The enemy gunner's round missed.

Bolan circled the bulky mass of the replica reactor, made a quick check of the tower to find its window still empty and moved back to the vestibule and hallway he'd emerged from. He ran its length, southward, made a quick jog to the west and spotted figures beginning to roll along the top of the wall in some type of vehicles. He spotted them first and stopped to fire carefully at the first group of three men. One flopped out of sight, his face ripped to shreds. The second began to raise his assault rifle to fire, but probably never even spotted Bolan before the second and third rounds ripped through his upper body. The third hardman flattened and was gone.

The Executioner ran in his direction, cutting to the left into another hallway until he came to the outside wall. Through the crudely hewn and lashed-together segments of wood, he could plainly see the van that was moving slowly along the outside wall. He also glimpsed the head and torso of the gunman as he rose to a crouch to look for his enemy.

Bolan placed the muzzle of the Desert Eagle in a large gap in the wood, and waited for the van to idle into range, then fired one time, less than two feet from the head of the driver. The force of the round punched the driver on his side, dead. The van lurched to the left and collided with the wall of the structure, tilting it. The gunner crouched on the roof was flung off, and he arced almost directly over the soldier's head before dropping to the earth like a sack of sticks.

The Executioner hoisted himself over the tilted fence and vaulted into the van, kicking the dead driver out of the way and wrenching the steering wheel in the other direction. He trod on the gas while unleathering the Beretta and firing several rounds in the direction of the other vehicles and hardmen on foot in the vicinity.

Bolan swapped hands, aimed the van at the nearby bunkhouse and fired out the driver's window, scattering the team that had gathered to storm the wooden structure from the front. He sent a few more shots up at the tower for good measure, then holstered his pistol and grabbed the pocketed stick of dynamite, quickly covering the distance to the largest compound building, the centrally located bunkhouse-garage. The front end of the van crashed through a lower-level wall and window of the bunkhouse, the wooden building giving way like kindling and the van coming to an abrupt halt half-embedded in a small bedroom.

Bolan bit off a length of the fuse and used a lighter from his backpack to start it. He propelled himself through a smashed-out front window, letting the dynamite stick bounce to the floor of the van. He somersaulted in the rubble and glass, ignoring the tearing of his skin and clothing, and crawled out of the room into the interior of the bunkhouse. A Malaysian man was at the far end of the hallway, looking at Bolan and the room with openmouthed surprise, which turned to slack-jawed shock when the ball of flame blasted out of the room and through the walls. The Malaysian was slammed into the wall and lay still where he had fallen.

Bolan embraced the floor and let the explosion billow over him, rolling quickly in case his hair or clothing had ignited, getting to his feet the instant the hot cloud dissipated. He had to find his way to the lower levels, to the garage beneath the building. There was no guarantee that the garage was where the plastique had been stored, but it was his best hunch. Jumping over the Malaysian who had been knocked cold by the blast, he ran to the west end of the building and found the stairs he was looking for. He came to locked double doors at the bottom of the landing and blasted the lock with a silenced burst from the Beretta 93-R.

As anticipated, Bolan found himself in a loading bay, lit by a few barred windows high in the ceiling—ground level to the earth next to the building. The drive that led to the surface was sloped sharply, and a garage door was closed and padlocked. He inspected the large garage, which included another flatbed pickup truck, but quickly determined there were no explosives stored there.

The soldier followed another hallway near the rear of the garage and found himself in utter darkness. He took the chance of using his flashlight and illuminated a tomblike concrete room, cramped and wet, with a single steel door set in the wall. He tried the door, which was locked. He put his flashlight to the tiny, barred window.

"Who's there?"

A face loomed in the yellowy beam, haggard, pasty and malnourished. Bolan knew him instantly. "Sellers."

"How do you know my name? Do I know you?"

"No. Fallen on hard times with CLAAC?"

The man grinned feebly, then withdrew into the darkness as if ashamed. The light revealed that Steven Sellers was in a wheelchair. "I'm sick."

"Radiation caused?"

"Yes. Lung cancer, as near as I can tell. A cruel irony for a nuclear scientist, isn't it?"

Bolan didn't comment. He doubted the families of the former employees of this man—those who were sick and had died as a result of his careless laboratory practices— would call that irony cruel. More likely their word would be *just*.

"Anyway, I had second thoughts. The first time in my life, but I actually did have second thoughts. Lung's going to make *so many* people very, very sick."

"Lung's got one last shipment of plastique. It isn't in the plane. Do you know where it is?"

"Yes, of course. He tells me everything. I'm a part of the CLAAC family."

"Where is it?"

"Not here. In fact, not in this building."

"Where?"

Sellers paused, looking into the darkness. "I won't tell you where it is, but I'll take you there. Then you have to take me with you when you blow this place. Got it?"

"If I take you with me, I'll be slowed down. I might not be able to blow those explosives at all."

"That's the only choice I'm offering you. If you think you can find them on your own, then go ahead. But I guarantee that without my help you'll never get to them."

Bolan didn't have a chance to consider before he heard the sound of activity in the garage. There were shouts and stomping feet—the enemy had discovered the shot-away door lock. A rhythm of footsteps told him three or four men were coming down the hall after him, and he opened fire. A scream of pain came from the garage, and a man tumbled out of the darkness. He heard men panicking in the garage, running for cover. They would gather their courage soon enough, Bolan knew.

He pointed the gun through the bars at Sellers.

"Where are the explosives?"

"Go ahead and shoot me. CLAAC will make sure I'm dead before they vacate the premises, you think I don't know that? Go ahead and rob them of the satisfaction."

Bolan pulled the gun away and blasted the lock, and the steel door swung open with creaking hinges. The shouts in the garage were getting louder.

"We'll never get out that way!" Sellers warned.

"It's our only option." Bolan stepped to the hall, grabbed the Type 56 assault rifle from the dead man and cut loose with a sizzling burst of rounds. The bullets bounced off the hallway walls, scattering the Chinese but doing no damage. It wouldn't slow them long.

"This is our way out," Sellers said, pointing to an opening in the wall next to the door to the cell. "It leads outside. You could go and pull me after you. We can use my blanket as a rope."

Bolan examined the ventilation shaft. It was only five feet off the ground and wide enough for him to shimmy through. He knew this route was a gamble, maybe even a desperate one, but there wasn't any other option.

He grabbed the thin, dank blanket from Sellers's bunk and instructed the man to wrap it around his back and under his arms, then pounded at the ventilation-shaft grate with the butt of the rifle, denting it the first two times, then knocking it off the wall. It clattered to the ground.

Bolan scrambled into the shaft and crawled through the skin-tight confines to the top grate, which looked out over a deserted patch of earth on the west side of the compound. He slammed the grate with his palm until it bent outward. Extricating himself, he dropped the rifle and went back into the shaft headfirst. The incline was slight, and he was able to wedge his knees against the walls of the shaft while he reached out and grabbed Sellers's hands, dragging him, bumping and pounding against the wall, into the shaft, with tremendous exertion.

"Hold yourself here!" Bolan ordered, and Sellers grabbed the walls of the shaft with his palms, terror scrawled in the sagging flesh of his face. The soldier crawled backward out of the shaft with the end of the blanket rope in his hand. He braced a foot against the wall and dragged on the rope, hoisting Sellers up out of the earth, seeing the man's frightened face ascend into view, his hands flailing for the opening and not quite able to reach it.

"Stop right there! And don't make a move for the gun!" Three men emerged from either side of the building, machine guns directed at Bolan, who didn't move. A last man stepped into view behind the others, a grin stretching across his face, and it could only be Hank Chiang.

The man laughed again, and his six gunmen stepped back and came together in a straight line, five paces away, distinctly resembling a firing squad.

Chiang stepped closer to Bolan. "Hands up. Drop that." Bolan dropped the blanket. In the shaft Sellers began to whimper. He couldn't hold himself in that position for long. "We meet again. I never did get your name, Mr.... ? No matter. Thanks for saving my life back in the U.S. Sorry I had to leave you there. Oh, well."

Sellers made a noise of helplessness and attracted Chiang's attention.

"Steve! There you are. We've been looking all over for you."

"Chiang," Bolan said, "why are you doing this?"

"Doing what?"

"The operation. The Fire Hammer. Why kill so many of your own people?"

"Ha! Do you know what our target is?"

"Daya Bay?"

"Yes, of course it is Daya Bay! Do you know what will happen when our bomb goes off?"

"I've considered it."

"Some will die—"

"Some?"

"Shut up! Some will die immediately, of course. A few hundred in the vicinity, perhaps. But that's not the point, is it? Several thousand more will be dosed with radiation big time!"

"Several hundred thousand. Perhaps several million."

"Including the people of Hong Kong, the heads of some of the biggest and most influential corporations on the planet. And some of the most globally influential. In fact, some of my own, close personal friends. And when they start to sicken and face their mortality, who will they blame?"

"The Western corporations who participated in the design of Daya Bay."

"No! They'll blame the PRC! What we're creating is the biggest negative-publicity campaign in all history." He laughed hysterically, eyes glazed. "But you want to stop me. And you!"

He turned to the air shaft, where Sellers was near to weeping with exertion. "You said you were going to help me, but then you changed your mind. I hate that!" He grabbed the blanket rope and dragged Sellers to the opening with surprising strength. The scientist's hands ejected from the opening, and he vainly flopped them about, as if afflicted with a horrible palsy, in a desperate attempt to extricate himself. "You let me down in a big way, Steve. You really, really let me down."

Chiang wrapped the blanket rope around Sellers's wrists and around his neck, effectively making him helpless in a few short seconds, and withdrew a lighter. "I really hate it when people do that. I really really hate it." There was a spark, then a tiny flame in his hands, and Bolan saw Sellers's eyes go wide with renewed terror. Chiang touched the flame to the blanket, which flared up, igniting Sellers's hair. Chiang put his foot on the burning man and shoved him back. A scream, and a dark cloud of acrid smoke, issued from the shaft.

Chiang threw back his head and laughed in delight.

16

Bolan snatched Chiang's open collar and pulled the man's body between himself and the six Chinese, in that instant drawing the Desert Eagle and placing its muzzle firmly against his hostage's cheek.

"Stop! Don't fire! Don't fire!" Chiang blurted frantically to both Bolan and his own men.

"That's right," the soldier said, "don't fire. Not yet." Chiang, he noticed, was no longer laughing. Keeping the muzzle of the .44 magnum pistol in place, he lifted his dropped rifle with his foot and grabbed it with his free hand. He placed the barrel into Chiang's back and moved the Desert Eagle to the base of his skull.

"You can't hurt me! You can't. They'll kill you if you hurt me."

"They'll kill me anyway. I'm not afraid of dying. Are you, Chiang? Why don't we go together?"

"No. You can still get out of here alive. Let me go, and I'll see to it you get out of here alive."

"Where's the plastique Chiang?"

"What?" He seemed truly confused. "Very funny. You can't seriously think you'll be able to get to the plastique."

"Sure, I can. Or we both die trying. Where is it?"

"It's in the hangar!"

"You're lying. I've been there."

"It's there—you've got to believe me. In a storage area under the floor! Now let me go."

Bolan believed him. If he'd only had the chance to search the hangar... He felt a surge of frustration.

"All right, Chiang, go." He planted his foot firmly in the small of the Chinese businessman's back and shoved him directly at the six gunmen. As the enemy fumbled for weapons, he squeezed the triggers on his two weapons. The Desert Eagle retorted powerfully, the assault rifle stuttering. With a broad sweep he raked a sustained burst over them, taking out the men on either end of the line first and working his way to the center from both sides.

"No!" Chiang howled, knowing he was a dead man, yet still diving to the ground. It was too late. Even as he was going down, his own gunmen returned Bolan's gunfire desperately and instead peppered Chiang with rounds from their own weapons. The Executioner ignored him and kept firing, blasting at the still-erect shapes of the Chinese gunmen. The din was a fog that seemed to surround him, and yet he barely noticed it. And finally, when the Desert Eagle clicked on empty, the soldier became aware that none of his adversaries was left standing. Somehow he still was. The suddenness of his attack had caught them by surprise, and his luck had held up.

Chiang was writhing on the ground, turning to look at Bolan with eyes filled with blood that seeped up from inside his body. The Executioner fired a mercy round from the the rifle and walked away.

Sounds of activity were coming from the north side of the compound. Bolan's goal was now the hangar anyway, to the southwest. He cut around the south side of the building and encountered a group of three Chinese coming around the far side of the building, a hundred yards distant. He fired several rounds from the assault rifle, only to feel it cycle dry. He fell to the ground against the building and dragged out the Beretta, a shot burst sending two men sprawling. The last man made a desperate belly-crawl to safety. Bolan let him go and sat up, making quick work of reloading the Desert Eagle.

"Hey, American."

The Executioner dived flat again, leveling the .44 Magnum pistol before the words died in the air, only to find he faced a barred window half-covered by grass. A dirty face peered out, fists on the bars. "I am unarmed!" the man cried.

Bolan rose into a crouch. "Who are you?"

"There are many of us. We are all from Ompang and from other places in Malaysia. We are imprisoned by the Chinese."

"Why?"

"Various reasons. Whenever we get too nosy, mostly. Or whenever we threaten to tell someone what is going on here at Siah. Or whenever the Chinese think we are going to tell someone what is going on here, we end up in prison."

Bolan hadn't relaxed his grip on the Desert Eagle, and he waved the muzzle. "Step back from the window."

The Malaysian pulled away, and Bolan shone the beam of his flashlight inside.

He saw what must have been thirty men, ragged and dirty. The stench that wafted through the bars was the smell of men living in their own filth.

"We'll help you, American," said their English-speaking spokesman. "Get us free, and we'll help you however we can."

Bolan began scrounging in his pack. He didn't really have time or the resources for a jailbreak. On the other hand... He didn't analyze his motivation. He just did it. "I'm going to blow the window. Turn away, get down, cover your faces." He planted the grenade in the grass, pulled the pin and raced down the side of the building in the direction he'd come. He ducked around the corner just as the blast echoed through the compound. Within seconds he had gathered the six assault rifles from the piled corpses of the dead hardmen and returned to the scene of the blast.

He'd calculated closely enough. Part of the ceiling of the floor above had been taken out by the blast, as well as a fairly decent crater in the earth, but the men inside had suffered only minor cuts and abrasions and were crawling through the rubble to freedom.

"Here." Bolan flung a rifle to the young man who spoke English. "Can you work that?"

"Yes, sir."

"Anybody else?" He raised the gun above his head.

The Malaysians understood the gesture if not the words. Half the men raised their hands, and Bolan distributed the weapons. "Come on. I need backup and you're elected."

"Sure, American." The young man yelled a brief order, and the entire troupe started after him. They headed directly south, across the landing strip and into the grass and bushes, and from there they could see the various pockets of activity. Most of it had presumably been at the front of the bunkhouse building, but the blast had caught CLAAC's attention, and men, Chinese and Malaysian both, were pouring around the building sides and in the direction of the escapees and Bolan.

"Keep them out of our hair," the soldier ordered. The young man shouted to his comrades as he was raising his own gun, and the rifle sputtered in his grip. One of the Chinese fell and the group of them halted. The other Malaysians in Bolan's group began to fire at them, and the Chinese didn't waste much time trying to figure out where they'd gotten their weapons before scrambling for cover.

Bolan was lying low and making his way through the vegetation, hoping to remain unseen while the Malaysians kept the CLAAC army occupied. He had to get through a hundred and twenty yards of low, bushy vegetation, then across another seventy yards of open ground before reaching the hangar, and as yet he'd formulated no plan for doing so.

There were shouts and cries from across the compound, and Bolan took out his field glasses. Under the lights around the replica control tower, he watched a large group of Chinese gathering around Kao Lung. The man was talking quickly and gesturing to the cars. When he'd finished, the CLAAC hardmen rushed to the vehicles. They drove the entire motor pool across the compound to the runway. Several cars and trucks were stationed on the runway, four more pulled into the open area on the side of the hangar, facing the vegetation with headlights blazing. Lung had established a perimeter of defense around the structure. There was no way Bolan was going to get through that.

Meanwhile, he'd seen Kao Lung head back to the building he assumed was the headquarters and living quarters for the CLAAC leaders. Bolan thought fast. If he couldn't get at the plastique, the essential tool in the Fire Hammer operation, then he would try to destroy the brains and driver behind it. He'd eradicated Chiang. Lung was all that was left.

The soldier descended into the vegetation and retraced his path to the west, behind the band of Malaysian prisoners, who were conserving their ammunition while the CLAAC army stayed their ground.

"I may have reinforcements coming," Bolan told the English-speaking youth. "If you can keep protecting yourselves until they arrive, they might be able to draw the attention away from you. But I have no idea when they'll be getting here or if they'll actually come with enough fire-power to do good.''

"Where you going, American?"

"To find Kao Lung."

"Nice knowing you."

He left them in their protected spot in the vegetation and moved on toward the eastern end of the compound, where the plant cover became much more dense. Bolan crouched and crawled deep in the wet, dank, muddy jungle and wormed unseen past the CLAAC vehicles that had circled around the far side of the bunkhouse and planted a perimeter there, as well.

The Chinese on the runway were exposed to him as he came alongside them, and he felt the itch to take out as many as he could. He could do extensive damage to the CLAAC ranks in about thirty seconds from his position, but the move would draw attention to him and would be counterproductive in the end.

So he sneaked around the rear force by heading almost to the front end of the compound, and managed to stay buried in darkness and vegetation all the way to the road. He bolted across the open asphalt and into the jungle beyond, but soon faced the wide-open area between the trees and the CLAAC headquarters.

Bolan surveyed the layout of the place as best he could, spotting a Malaysian guard at the front door and several others scattered around the outside of the building. A single Chinese guard was in evidence, stationed on the roof and making slow rounds on all sides, though mostly trying to make out what was happening in the various pockets of activity around the compound.

One of the vehicles from the standoff with the Malaysian escapees roared around the bunkhouse and headed in the direction of the headquarters. Several Chinese exited the truck and spoke curtly to the Malaysian guard, who remained where he was. A few of the Chinese began circling the building, calling to the Malaysian guards in English, their shared tongue, ordering them to gather on the covered front porch of the building. A CLAAC member entered the building and came out a moment later with five more Malaysians. In minutes there were twenty Malaysians standing before the building, waiting.

Kao Lung stepped out of the front door of the headquarters building.

"I have new orders for yourself and your men. Something unlike your previous assignments. Something that won't be as boring as guard duty."

Lung aimed his handgun directly at the Malaysian's stomach. Bolan saw the Malaysian captain looking confused, but this was allayed as soon as he saw all his men being relieved of their weapons by the Chinese at gunpoint.

"What is this, Mr. Lung?"

"We simply can't trust you and your men anymore. There's a volatile situation in progress here. Many Malaysian prisoners have escaped. We might have to kill them."

"So what?"

"We don't want to get you and your men involved and risk them becoming sympathetic with the prisoners."

"They are good fighters!"

"Of course they are. You and your men have served us well in recent months. And we appreciate your help. But we feel it best if we keep you out of the fight now. We have only a few more short hours to go. Then we'll be gone and you'll have your money."

"What are you going to do with us?"

"We're going to round up the Malaysians in the compound and keep you all in the reactor for the rest of the dark hours. Before dawn we'll all be gone, and you'll be free to do as you please.''

Lung's voice was controlled and soothing, and the captain, despite obvious doubts, didn't protest further. He handed his weapon to Lung, who lowered the muzzle of his own handgun as an act of good faith. They marched away in the direction of the replica reactor. The CLAAC leader left them and reentered the building.

Bolan saw his chance to take care of the man on the roof. He'd watched the proceedings with the Malaysians without changing his expression, then wandered clockwise around the rim of the building. In a minute he'd make another appearance.

The Executioner fired the Beretta, but in that instant fate made an effort to save the man. A burst of gunfire erupted on the far side of the bunkhouse. The man jerked his head, and the 9 mm parabellum round flew past his head. A split second later his eyes locked on Bolan. By then the soldier was firing again. The guard opened his mouth to scream, and the bullet ripped through his Adam's apple and trachea. His scream came out as a rush of air and bubbling blood. Then the guard crumpled to his knees and fell on his side out of sight.

Bolan rushed across the open space and entered the building through the front door, finding himself in a carpeted hallway, which was air-conditioned and dry compared to the humid, tropical atmosphere outside. Chiang's doing, he guessed.

He closed the door behind him and exchanged the Beretta for the Desert Eagle. Through the partially opened door of the first room he came to, he saw a large, comfortable chair among the other furniture, and dozing in it was Thomas Comas. On the table next to him was an empty glass and bottle of whiskey, almost empty. The alcohol smell in the air was powerful.

He heard voices and followed the sound to another, larger room. Glancing in, he saw the corner of what appeared to be a large conference table. An unfamiliar Chinese figure lounged in a chair, listening to the speaker, who Bolan recognized as Lung.

The soldier stepped to the door and kicked it open, aiming before he knew the layout of the room at the voice he knew was Lung's. But fate saved the man's life—he had stepped behind a thick column of wood, one of several along the far side of the large room. The .44 Magnum round from the Desert Eagle blasted away a chunk of the wood, and the CLAAC leader collapsed to the floor, blood erupting from his head, but Bolan knew he'd been hit only superficially.

There was a shuffling sound from all sides, and Bolan triggered on the others in the room, a half-dozen or more Chinese. A man had been standing near the back of the room with an assault rifle, and he was the first to appear to achieve target acquisition with his weapon. Bolan took him out with the Desert Eagle, then fired at the nearest man, who was bringing up a small handgun. The massive round drilled through the man's forehead, punching him backward before dumping him on the floor.

The Executioner caught the movement of a side door, not far from where Lung collapsed, and watched the disappearance of a black-clad leg. The CLAAC leader had made an escape on all fours.

With a cursory look to make sure the way was clear, Bolan jumped to his feet and went in pursuit of Kao Lung.

17

Jiahua and Qiu ran off the main Ompang road into a side street. The woman flattened against a wooden house, glancing around the corner cautiously while her companion waited expressionlessly. She grinned at him, wondering if he was really stoic or just good at hiding his excitement, because she was exhilarated.

She whipped around the corner, scanning the area, searching for a target. Nothing.

"Where the hell did he go?"

"I do not know."

"It was a rhetorical question anyway." She waved forward, and they ran through the backyards of a string of small huts, startling the chickens. The locals were nowhere to be seen. They had heard the gunfire and taken cover in their homes.

They came to an end to the yards, and Jiahua found herself in familiar territory. Yes, there was the trail into the jungle, which they had taken earlier that day to the compound in the Siah Canyon.

Then she noticed the boy.

It was Kin, who had shown them the path, the one who had used her coins to purchase a bicycle. He was lying on a table on the back porch of the last house, dressed in clean, neatly pressed clothes, and his black hair was carefully

combed. But his skin was blackened and his closed ey
puffy and dark.

"Oh, no."

"What?" Qiu asked.

Jiahua stopped at the edge of the porch and gazed at th
boy—dead, doubtless because he had helped them.

"Jiahua."

"Just a second."

She touched Kin's hand, then turned away from him.

The Chinese hardman emerged from his cover in the jungle four paces behind her, leveled an old Australian F-1 machine gun at her back and pulled the trigger.

Jiahua never heard him. But she saw Qiu yank his rifle to his shoulder, watched the barrel orient so precisely on her head she thought she could peer all the way down the barrel and heard the retort of the weapon so quickly she didn't have time to do anything more than wonder why her comrade had suddenly decided to assassinate her.

But the bullet whistled past her ear, and she heard a grunt and a clatter of machine-gun fire. She plummeted to the earth, turning to see the gunner in the brush falling to the ground on his back and firing into the treetops. She got to her feet again, stunned at how close she had come to death. Shredded leaves were falling from the trees like ticker tape.

"You're welcome," Qiu said.

Jiahua nodded. Her lips moved to make the words *thank you,* but no sound came out.

There was another noise, however, that caught her attention—the sound of chickens being disturbed a couple of houses away. Her eyes met Qiu's, and they started through the gap between the houses, glancing around the corner. She spotted a Chinese man with a big gun, who turned and fled in the other direction.

ay.'' She pointed around the next row of
ook off. Qiu circled the building and
rallel to her, ready to spot the CLAAC
he duck through to the right.

as having trouble keeping the enemy gunner
He was in dark clothing, and the night was black.

pang's social services didn't include street lighting, or streets for that matter. She glimpsed him five houses ahead as he ducked to the right, then to the left.

"Qiu!" she called.

The Chinese agent was running parallel with her between the next row of houses. "I don't see him!"

She ducked to the left herself, between houses, and looked carefully around the corner. Nothing. Had he veered to the left? If he'd gone right, wouldn't Qiu have spotted him? She stepped into the open, aiming her pistol, spotting nothing and proceeding. She jumped on the porch of the dark house and stepped quietly to the corner, half-expecting to come face-to-face with the CLAAC hardman. She stood against the wall and heard nothing. Waving her hand around the corner elicited no response. Where was this guy?

Jiahua finally peered around the corner. The place between the buildings was empty, and she nearly cursed out loud before covering the distance to the right again with a quick jog and looking back the way she'd just come. Nothing. It was possible that the man had invaded one of the houses.

Growing fearful of another hostage situation, she sprinted across the open space and confessed her suspicion to her partner.

"Then he might be anywhere. In any house."

"Yeah, and how do we figure out which one? Knock on doors?"

"Why are these men heading in this direction anyway?" Qiu asked.

Jiahua had the answer to that one. "Because they know about the trail," she stated. "They knew it is the only safe way back to the compound—they'd be wary of the road. They must be trying to reach it on their own after getting separated from their units during our raid. Come on!"

She bolted back to the backyards where the jungle and the trail began, Qiu close on her heels. They stopped at the edge of the house and peered into the backyard. Their first CLAAC victim lay where he'd fallen.

"No living soul," Qiu stated.

"But does that mean he's made it here behind our backs? Or have we beat him here?"

Her comrade shrugged. "How can we know?"

HE WAS EXHAUSTED and disillusioned. So many of his comrades captured or dead! And he'd nearly been shot dead a half-dozen times himself, most recently by a woman. His face burned with shame, for himself and for his friends.

But mostly he was worried about the fate of the leaders of his organization. Were they being attacked simultaneously? Or was the Malaysian strike force, even now scouring Ompang, planning to move on to the Siah Canyon compound next? If only he could reach them and warn them!

He had to try.

He knew where the trail was, knew it passed for several miles through the jungle before emptying onto the road into the Siah Canyon. What he didn't know was its travel time. On foot could he reach the entrance to the canyon fast enough to warn Kao Lung and Hang Chiang?

He had to try.

He seemed to have eluded the Chinese woman. He suspected she was of Chinese parentage only, and that she was actually an agent for the U.S. or Malaysian government.

Whoever she was, he hated her for being the enemy of the forces that would free China, hated her because she had shamed him by almost getting the better of him. No woman belonged in a place of power over a man, and that was one of the imbalances of totalitarian government that CLAAC's new order would provide for.

Reaching the spot where the trail began, he hid behind a building and looked for the woman and for her companion, the one with the powerful rifle.

He saw no living thing. But he did see two dead men. One was a boy—that was only the boy they had beat this afternoon. His family had laid him out. He was of no consequence.

The second body was a member of CLAAC. He lay on his back, gun in hand, a hole gaping in his chest and his legs folded uncomfortably underneath him. Somehow he was a symbol of what had happened to CLAAC here this night. Ambush and shame.

There was no time to mourn him or any of his lost comrades. One day they would be called heroes. He stepped across the open space and into the jungle.

The vegetation closed in, dark and oppressive.

He had hiked several hundred yards into the jungle, Ompang receding into the darkness and foliage, when he heard an animal's voice behind him.

He turned and fired, creating chaos among the leaves of the ferns and low-lying plantlife. Listening intently for a moment afterward, he heard nothing and told himself that whatever it had been the creature had turned tail and wouldn't be bothering him again.

His march resumed. The rain forest became blacker. The roof above became solid. What few slivers of night sky he glimpsed transmitted no light down to him. He couldn't even see well enough to be sure he was still on the trail.

Then there was movement off to his right, and he opened up with the assault rifle, allowing the magazine to cycle dry. Then bullets started flying at him. He couldn't tell where they were coming from, but he knew he was dead even in that instant. He could feel them. He'd been tricked into revealing his position, making himself a target in the pitch-blackness.

The hardman fell to the ground with that thought, his last.

Jiahua approached the Chinese, kicking the gun out of his grip.

Qiu stepped out of the bushes and looked down at the corpse. His shots were well grouped in its chest. The man was quite dead.

They headed back to the village to help finish cleaning it up.

BOLAN WENT through the back door, squeezing the trigger on the Desert Eagle before he knew what lay beyond, and blasted through a closing door at the other end of a narrow, empty room. He sprinted out the door, finding himself outside, facing the northern cliff wall. He peripherally noticed movement to the right and fell to the ground as shots rang over his head. The soldier fired at the car that concealed the gunner, keeping the man pinned, giving himself time to scramble to his feet and run at the car. The Chinese finally dared to peek over the hood of the vehicle only to find his adversary standing ten feet away and targeting him at close range. Bolan fired, and the gunman dropped.

He grabbed the Uzi from the dead man and made his way carefully around the front of the headquarters, looking for Lung, though he was sure the man had fled. The front door opened, and Thomas Comas came out, searching furtively and drunkenly for the source of the gunfire that had interrupted his alcoholic nap. He was awkwardly waving a .38 Special. Comas noticed Bolan and ducked behind the front door again, then smashed a small window in the door with the handgun and fired six wild shots before clicking on empty chambers.

The Executioner leveled the Uzi at the door and fired directly into the wood five times. He yanked at the door, and Thomas Comas's corpse flopped out.

The giant wooden reactor replica stood adjacent, and a large group of men trudged inside the building. It was clear the men going inside the replica were Malaysian, and they were being held at gunpoint by several Chinese. The CLAAC terrorists were getting ready for departure from Malaysia, and Bolan knew only a few witnesses would be left behind. He understood now the real purpose of the hundreds of sticks of dynamite hidden in the middle of the false reactor.

He charged across the open area to the reactor, firing the Uzi on the run. The helpless, unarmed Malaysians recoiled against the wooden wall, sinking to the ground or scrambling inside the wooden structure. The Chinese searched out the source of the fire and targeted Bolan quickly. He shot two of the hardmen in the chest, then dropped into a somersaulted roll as if tripped, letting a volley of gunfire burn the air where he had been standing. He landed flat on his stomach in the grass and cut loose. The stream of bullets from the Uzi rattled into the Chinese, jerking them into a macabre dance of death before they collapsed to the ground.

He got to his feet and turned to the Malaysians. "Anybody speak English?"

There were looks of dismay among the men, none of them understanding. There was more gunfire beyond the bunkhouse, and Bolan wondered how well his prisoner friend was doing as he made his stand in the vegetation with his escapee comrades.

A four-wheel-drive screeched from behind the CLAAC headquarters building at top speed and slammed to a stop thirty yards away. Gunfire erupted from the passenger-side window, and Bolan immediately determined it was designed to get the Malaysians into the replica reactor. He fired at the vehicle, a black mass in the night, hoping to score on the driver, and heard the reassuring sound of smashing glass. The fire from the vehicle halted, and he saw the figure sticking out the window draw inside suddenly. He aimed carefully for the driver and shot four more rounds. The vehicle's headlights came on and just as suddenly winked out, shattered by rounds from Bolan's Desert Eagle. Then the vehicle spun in a backward half circle and screeched away in the direction of the hangar.

But the attack had achieved its purpose. The Malaysians were rushing for cover inside the reactor. Bolan had to do something about it. He was convinced Lung was planning to remotely trigger the dynamite in the fake reactor core, killing as many of the Malaysians as he could.

Bolan ran into the midst of the pushing horde and managed to fight his way through the front entrance of the replica into the dark maze beyond. He had been there, and a mental blueprint guided his direction. But the Malaysians were making their way through the structure, as well, hoping somehow to find a back entrance or a way of escape. He pushed past the milling throng, eliciting Malay profanity, guiding himself through the halls and rooms.

When he burst into the large, open reactor room, Bolan found twenty-five men already there. A few were trying to scale the fifteen-foot high back wall and as yet had not succeeded. The soldier ran to the middle of the room, to the large, wooden bulk of the fake reactor, and grabbed at a piece of the hewn-wood exterior.

Several of the men spoke to him in Malay and looked at him curiously. Bolan urged them to help him, hoping his meaning would be clear. A few gathered in his vicinity, and he called to them again. Then the board came loose in his hand, and he flung it away. Another came off quickly. He was getting more leverage, and he ripped five or six of the boards off and discarded them.

Before him was a framework of steel bars holding row upon row of dynamite sticks.

He ripped off several more of the boards, high above his head. He assumed the detonation device was radio-controlled, probably designed to be set off from the hangar; therefore, the receiver would be set high in the simulated reactor. He glimpsed a metal box and began tearing away the boards in its vicinity, quickly trying to gain access to it, while in the very back of his brain he was trying to guess how long Lung would wait before triggering the dynamite. He would wait until most of the Malaysians were inside and his men were at a safe distance. But the Malaysians were nearly all inside now, and the Chinese hardmen had been killed or driven back. Bolan had to admit, when he considered it logically, that there was no reason for Lung to wait one second longer.

He ripped another board from the framework, flinging it behind him, and reached through with his hand, feeling the cool metal of the radio receiver against his fingertips. He could do no more than touch it. Pulling his arm out, he wrenched off more boards for better access, and in the back of his mind he wondered what would occur in the moment the receiver received its signal. Would there be a click from the detonator? A flash? A small explosion to trigger the full-scale explosion? He bodily yanked back on the last board, and the nails that held it in place squealed against the wooden frame, held for an instant, then popped free on one end. He didn't bother yanking it off fully, but thrust his arm into the opening, slamming his shoulder against the frame. The bent loose nails of the boards scraped through his clothing into the flesh of his back, and he felt the cool metal receiver the size of a cellular telephone fall into his grip. He yanked it out of the reactor and found it was attached to a single stick of dynamite. The explosion of a single stick was more than sufficient to trigger the explosion of the hundreds of sticks in the reactor. A red light silently lit on the receiver and Bolan flung the thing against the front wall of the reactor room.

The receiver flared and exploded just before it hit the earth. The air thundered with the percussive blast, and a gaping hole was ripped through the wall.

Bolan got to his feet. Several of the Malaysians had been knocked off their feet and were covered with abrasions from the splintered wood. But their looks and lightning-fast conversation told him they were realizing what had just occurred. They looked at the mound of dynamite with something like awe.

"Come on," Bolan said. "Help me out." He began grabbing at the dynamite, filling his arms with the sticks. The Malaysians were unsure. "Come on!" he ordered. Finally several of them started taking the sticks gingerly. Soon they had cleaned out the framework of the reactor. Bolan estimated they had 225 sticks.

He led the men to the front of the reactor, where he directed the unloading of the dynamite into one of the abandoned cars, a boxy station wagon. Bolan took a belt from one of the men and tied it to the steering wheel but didn't yet secure the end. He would need to steer the vehicle into position.

There were shouts from the men, and Bolan looked up to see four vehicles driving in through the front entrance of the compound. In the darkness he couldn't be certain, but as they passed under the lights at the entrance he saw they were painted camouflage. He wondered if they might be reinforcements and if so, for which side.

He crouched on the far side of the station wagon as the cars approached. The Malaysians milled about uncertainly, then their hands started going up in the air as if in surrender. Jiahua and Qiu emerged from the first troop transport.

"Belasko!" she shouted when he showed himself.

"I see you've found help."

"Yeah. Malaysian army. We ran CLAAC out of Ompang. Half of them fled south, deeper into the jungle. The rest are dead or in the hands of the people of Ompang. What's going on here?"

"Chiang's dead. Lung and most of the Chinese are in the hangar. I think they're getting ready to leave. I'm going to stop them."

"By yourself? How?"

He waved to the rear window of the station wagon, with its cargo of dynamite. She whistled low and long.

"How can we help? We've got four army vehicles and forty troops. Not much, but it was all they had available in the vicinity."

Bolan nodded. "What do you have in the way of hardware?"

Jiahua spoke to the Malaysian captain, who quickly opened up the rear end of his transport.

The troops inside were equipped with unexceptional army gear but there was a selection of special-duty equipment. He saw what he wanted—a box marked in English. It was a U.S. LAW rocket launcher.

"I'll take this."

The captain of the Malaysian team objected vigorously. Jiahua argued with him, then Qiu stepped in. His voice was quick and to the point. Bolan didn't know what he said, but it did the trick. The Malaysian captain relented. The Executioner grabbed the rocket-launcher case.

"I'm going around the back way to try to plant these explosives in the hangar with Lung's airplane. You go around the front end of that building and engage them. Keep them distracted."

"Got ya."

"Take these men with you. I think they'll be pretty willing to turn against their former employers after what CLAAC tried to do to them. Give them any weapons you've got."

"Why don't I come with you, Belasko?" Jiahua said. "There's more than enough Malays to keep the front end active. And you may need help."

"No, thanks. It'll be hard enough getting within close vicinity on my own."

"You know," she said, "sometimes two heads are better than one."

"Sometimes. Not this time."

"Fine."

18

The Malays were provided with the few extra weapons that could be scrounged up from the military vehicles, but that armed less than a dozen of them. There were forty Malay soldiers, plus Qiu and Jiahua.

They boarded the military transports and started off at a slow pace to the big bunkhouse, the throngs of Malays gathering behind them. Jiahua and the Chinese agent examined the ruin of the vehicle jutting out of the front of the bunkhouse, still smoking.

"Our friend?" Qiu wondered aloud.

The woman nodded. Surely this was his handiwork. What the hell had been happening here in the past few hours? She hoped he lived through this to tell her about it.

Withdrawing her Heckler & Koch MP-5 A-5, she checked her rounds, then withdrew the Colt All American Auto, removed the magazine, and ascertained she had a full fifteen shots and reinserted the magazine, which made a reassuring click. With a quick touch to the inside of her shin, she checked that her knife was in place. She was prepared for the battle to come.

Qiu was busily loading his sniper rifle.

"You're very good with that thing, aren't you?"

He met her eyes and inclined his head briefly. "You've seen my work. Yes, I am very good."

"I'd like you to stay out of the fray, maybe keep to the back. Keep an eye on the scene—Belasko, I mean. Us, too. Maybe you can help avert any trouble that might develop."

Qiu thought briefly, staring at the floor of the military vehicle. "Yes, I will do so."

The Malay captain spouted orders into the radio. The transports were about to pull around the side of the bunkhouse to face CLAAC.

BOLAN RACED the station wagon away from the wooden structure and was quickly within view of the closed hangar, which was still an appreciable distance away. Between himself and the hangar was a short stretch of grassy earth, the packed-dirt area of what had been used as the training grounds for the CLAAC terrorists, then the runway and the hangar.

He hit the gas and drove the vehicle onto the training grounds, noticing the sudden appearance of armed Chinese alongside the building.

The wide, garagelike door of the hangar began to pull open.

THE TRANSPORT HALTED, and Jiahua and Qiu jumped out, one on either side of the vehicle. She saw him retreat to the rear of the other transports as they halted in a line just off the runway. The Malay soldiers hopped out.

The MP-5 A-5 submachine gun was cool beneath the skin of her arm, reassuring and solid. Raising it, she assessed the situation—the three CLAAC vehicles faced the south wall of the canyon. There was a retort from the jungle that grew along the base of the canyon, and she heard the round hit one of the vehicles. The CLAAC gunners returned fire at the source of the shot, but it was only a seemingly empty spot in the vegetation.

Somebody was keeping the Chinese occupied, and they hadn't noticed the arrival of the newcomers until that instant. Then there was a shout among the Chinese, and the gunmen standing behind the CLAAC vehicles found themselves surrounded. Jiahua only had to see one of the men redirect his Uzi at her before she brought her own weapon into play, triggering the Heckler & Koch without conscious decision. The gunman flung his Uzi away and cracked his spine against his car.

The fight was bloody, and it became a battle within the space of seconds, the Malays and the Chinese exchanging ferocious gunfire. Jiahua found herself awash in a sense of near-peace. Nothing was out of control or chaotic or moving too fast for her now. She raised the submachine gun and directed its stream of fire at one Chinese hardman, and then another. The Malaysians were doing good work as well, and the woman heard the occasional, finely punctuated blast from Men Qiu's sniper rifle.

Soon the three vehicles were revving to life and fleeing in the direction of the hangar. Other CLAAC vehicles met up with the fleeing force. Jiahua assumed they were going to form a line of defense in the middle of the runway, but the cars and trucks all turned and headed for the hangar.

There were sounds of vehicles behind them, and the woman turned to face a new attack. Dammit, where had they come from? Another two cars were pulling into the compound—the last of the group that had been in Ompang looking for Belasko. She shouted orders to her Malaysian soldiers. They dived for safety and rose behind their transports firing, but the horde of unarmed Malaysians was out in the open.

Jiahua fired at the front vehicle and managed to take out the Chinese driver. Another hardman appeared from behind a second car and fired wildly. One of the unprotected

Malaysians dropped to the ground, but his Chinese killer didn't last long himself. There was a single retort from Qiu's rifle, and the gunman flopped to the ground.

Then the woman suddenly didn't know what was happening. There was a chaos of gunfire from the newcomers, but it was directed internally, not at the Malays or at the military force. There were Malays coming out of the vehicles, pointing their guns at their own comrades. Several CLAAC members were putting up a struggle, and Jiahua watched them get gunned down by their Malaysian companions. She shouted an order to her captain, who relayed the order to his own men. There was a silence and an air of potent anticipation before the Malays began marching toward them, guns raised in both hands above their heads, a very few surviving Chinese, disarmed and surrendering, preceding them at gunpoint.

The Malays from the compound rushed to their countrymen and were shouting angrily at the Chinese. Before she knew it, the Chinese were on the ground, surrounded by Malays. They were screaming for mercy as they were kicked and beaten. Jiahua wondered what CLAAC had done to the Malaysians to make them so angry. She sensed some sort of betrayal.

Her superiors at the CIA probably wouldn't have approved, but the agent chose not to interfere.

INSIDE THE HANGAR a metal section of the floor had been removed and lay discarded to the side, and underneath was a gaping pit. The last load of C-4 plastique had been in the hangar all along. Now it was in the plane; the door of the Lockheed Electra was closing even as the aircraft was moving.

Bolan's plan suddenly had only minutes to work or it would be too late. He trod hard on the gas pedal, and the

vehicle bolted across the training grounds. The nose of the
Electra was pushing out between the parting hangar doors
before they were even open wide enough to allow the aircraft's wings to pass through.

The Executioner wedged a piece of wood he'd grabbed
from the reactor between the seat and the gas pedal and
made quick work of lashing the leather belt around the
floor-mounted gearshift. The car bounced from the dirt
training ground and over a short stretch of grass. Bolan
flung open the door, grabbed the LAW case and shoved
himself out, hitting the grass and rolling as the car jolted
onto the edge of the runway, crossing it and passing underneath the left wing of the airplane. The station wagon had
veered to the right and entered the hangar interior, crashing
into the side wall.

The Electra pointed toward the far end of the runway and
increased speed quickly. A large number of CLAAC vehicles were headed from the scene of the bunkhouse battle,
roaring toward the hangar.

Bolan scrambled across the ground to the rocket-launcher
case, snatched the instrument from its foam compartment,
shoved in the first projectile and brought it to his shoulder
and eye. The Electra was still within twenty feet of the hangar. He sighted the station wagon and depressed the LAW's
launcher trigger, at the same instant watching the convoy of
Chinese pull in front of the building. The rocket soared
away from him on a path of gray smoke, crossing within two
yards of the first car. Bolan watched the projectile veering
off course, affected by the very air it passed through, and hit
the ground under the rear end of the wrecked station wagon,
where it erupted in fire. The front Chinese vehicle veered.

The hangar was replaced suddenly by a searing orange
ball of flame. The CLAAC vehicles disappeared inside of it,
like sand figures swallowed by a foaming ocean wave, and

Bolan hit the ground. The blast of superheated air washed over the landscape and burned his skin and heated his clothes, so that for a moment he thought he was on fire and rolled onto his back. By then the ball of flame was already receding. He pushed himself onto his feet, resting himself a second with his hands on his legs.

The Chinese convoy was gone, replaced by several heat-shrunken, blackened masses of debris, still flaming.

The Electra was black near the tail. If it had been on fire, the flames were out already. The plane appeared to be without serious damage.

It had reached the end of the runway and was making a 180 degree turn, pointing west. Most of the CLAAC terrorists were now dead. But enough of them—including Kao Lung, Bolan was sure—were aboard that airplane, little standing between them and the dark success of their Fire Hammer.

The pitch from the props rose, and the plane went into motion, starting its short taxi prior to takeoff. Bolan grabbed the remaining rocket from the case, placed it firmly into the launcher and sighted it. The gray smoke appeared again and the missile zipped through the open air before it veered off its direct flight, passing under the belly of the Electra, hitting the ground. The explosion cratered the earth and rocked the plane, but its acceleration continued. The plane passed Bolan, gaining speed rapidly.

The soldier tossed away the LAW and brought out the powerful Desert Eagle. His chances were growing slimmer by the millisecond. He sighted on the rear horizontal stabilizers of the aircraft and triggered the big pistol, the .44 Magnum rounds tearing into the stabilizer.

His shots began to miss as the aircraft's distance rapidly increased, but Bolan kept firing until the Desert Eagle clicked empty.

The soldier found himself in the middle of the runway, watching the airplane scatter the Malay military vehicles and take to the air. The Malays jumped from their cars and started firing at it themselves, but by then the plane was out of range.

The craft was airborne and gaining altitude. It maneuvered to the left slightly, dipping erratically. The horizontal stabilizer was failing to operate. The pilot attempted to compensate, but the plane wouldn't turn. The northern wall of the Siah Canyon was coming at it fast. The aircraft lurched to the left, but it wasn't compensation enough. The rear end of the Electra crashed into the mountain and was pulverized.

Bolan watched the airplane gain altitude, and for a moment thought it was somehow under control. It was a temporary illusion. The aircraft was helpless without its rear stabilizers. The airplane sped toward the earth, slamming into the jungle and exploding with a blast of white fire.

Bolan squinted against the bright light, his teeth clenched, and his lips in a grim line. He felt no true satisfaction, now that this mission had come to a fiery end. This was really a small battle in his Everlasting War.

The warrior turned his back on the conflagration and walked into the night.

Exiles from the future in the
aftermath of the apocalypse

JAMES AXLER

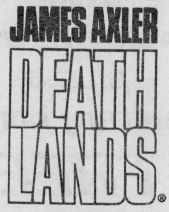

Stoneface

In 2001, the face of the earth changed forever in a nuclear
firestorm. Generations after the apocalypse, Ryan Cawdor leads
the courageous struggle for survival in a brutal world, striving to
make a difference in the battle raging between good and evil.

In the Deathlands, the war is over...but the fight has just begun.

Take
4 explosive books
plus a
mystery bonus
FREE

Mail to: Gold Eagle Reader Service
3010 Walden Ave.
P.O. Box 1394
Buffalo, NY 14240-1394

YEAH! Rush me 4 FREE Gold Eagle novels and my FREE mystery gift.
Then send me 4 brand-new novels every other month as they come off
the presses. Bill me at the low price of just $15.80* for each shipment—
a saving of 15% off the cover prices for all four books! There is NO extra
charge for postage and handling! There is no minimum number of books I
must buy. I can always cancel at any time simply by returning a shipment
at your cost or by returning any shipping statement marked "cancel." Even
if I never buy another book from Gold Eagle, the 4 free books and surprise
gift are mine to keep forever.

164 BPM A3U3

Name	(PLEASE PRINT)	
Address		Apt. No.
City	State	Zip

Signature (if under 18, parent or guardian must sign)

* Terms and prices subject to change without notice. Sales tax applicable in
NY. This offer is limited to one order per household and not valid to
present subscribers. Offer not available in Canada.

AC-96

**Killer rays from space threaten
to cook America's goose....**

THE Destroyer

#105 Scorched Earth

Created by
WARREN MURPHY
and RICHARD SAPIR

A single superheated zap from an invisible object in space literally vaporizes the Biobubble habitat scientists. More sizzling attacks are followed by eyewitness sightings of giant Cyrillic letters in the sky.

Look for it in December, wherever Gold Eagle books are sold.

A new warrior breed blazes
a trail to an uncertain future.

JAMES AXLER

DEATH LANDS ®

Bitter Fruit

In the nuclear-storm devastated Deathlands a warrior survivalist
deals with the serpent in a remote Garden of Eden.

Nature rules in the Deathlands, but man still destroys.

**Don't miss out on the action in these titles featuring
THE EXECUTIONER® and STONY MAN™!**

The Red Dragon Trilogy

#64210	FIRE LASH	$3.75 U.S. ☐
		$4.25 CAN. ☐
#64211	STEEL CLAWS	$3.75 U.S. ☐
		$4.25 CAN. ☐
#64212	RIDE THE BEAST	$3.75 U.S. ☐
		$4.25 CAN. ☐

Stony Man™

#61903	NUCLEAR NIGHTMARE	$4.99 U.S. ☐
		$5.50 CAN. ☐
#61904	TERMS OF SURVIVAL	$4.99 U.S. ☐
		$5.50 CAN. ☐
#61905	SATAN'S THRUST	$4.99 U.S. ☐
		$5.50 CAN. ☐
#61906	SUNFLASH	$5.50 U.S. ☐
		$6.50 CAN. ☐
#61907	THE PERISHING GAME	$5.50 U.S. ☐
		$6.50 CAN. ☐

(limited quantities available on certain titles)

TOTAL AMOUNT	$
POSTAGE & HANDLING	$
($1.00 for one book, 50¢ for each additional)	
APPLICABLE TAXES*	$
TOTAL PAYABLE	$
(check or money order—please do not send cash)	

To order, complete this form and send it, along with a check or money order for the total above, payable to Gold Eagle Books, to: **In the U.S.:** 3010 Walden Avenue, P.O. Box 9077, Buffalo, NY 14269-9077; **In Canada:** P.O. Box 636, Fort Erie, Ontario, L2A 5X3.

Name:_____

Address:_____ City:_____

State/Prov.:_____ Zip/Postal Code:_____

*New York residents remit applicable sales taxes.
Canadian residents remit applicable GST and provincial taxes.

GEBACK16